THE RANDOM HOUSE BOOK OF
HOW THINGS WORK

Editor: Thomas Keegan
Design: David West Children's
Book Design
Consultant: Rowena Knox
Index: Jane Parker

The publishers would like to thank
the following artists for contributing
to this book:

Graham Austin (The Garden Studio)
pp. 124–129; Peter Bull pp. 14–17,
18–27, 32–35, 40–43, 52–61, 108–
123, 134–145; Neil Bulpitt pp. 44–47,
86–99; Peter Gregory (Introductory
illustrations) pp. 44, 48, 62, 68, 74,
78, 82, 86, 92, 96, 104, 106; Aziz Khan
pp. 62–65, 68–73, 100–107;
Ian Moores pp. 36–39, 48–51, 74–85,
92–95, 130–133; Alex Pang, cover;
Rob Shone (Introductory
illustrations) pp. 15, 18, 24, 28, 32,
36, 40, 52, 56, 58, 108, 114, 116, 120,
130, 134, 138, 142.

First American edition, 1991

Library of Congress Cataloging-in-Publication Data:

Parker, Steve.
The Random House book of how things work / by Steve Parker.
p. cm.
Includes index.
Summary: A comprehensive, illustrated guide showing how more
than 300 machines, mechanisms, and processes that affect our
everyday lives work.
1. Technology—Juvenile literature. [1. Technology.] I. Title.
T48.P37 1991 90-9137 600—dc20
ISBN 0-679-80908-2 (trade); 0-679-90908-7 (lib. bdg.)

Manufactured in Italy

THE RANDOM HOUSE BOOK OF
HOW THINGS WORK

STEVE PARKER

Random House 🏠 New York

CONTENTS

BUILDING AND CONSTRUCTION

THE BUILDING SITE 52–55
UNDERGROUND SERVICES · DIGGER · TOWER CRANE
DRILLING AND PILEDRIVING · RIVETS AND WELDS
CONCRETE MIXER · SPIRIT LEVEL · ELEVATOR

BRIDGES 56–57
TYPES OF BRIDGES · SPANNING THE RIVER
NUTS AND BOLTS · THEODOLITE

TUNNELS 58–61
TUNNEL STRUCTURE · TUNNEL-BORING MACHINE
PISTON RELIEF DUCT · SUMP PUMP · DO-DO TRAIN
FIRE DETECTOR · FIRE EXTINGUISHER

POWER AND SERVICES

OIL EXPLORATION 62–67
RIGS AND PLATFORMS · DRILLING RIG
EXPLORATION RIG · DIVING EQUIPMENT
PRODUCTION PLATFORM · HELICOPTER

POWER STATIONS 68–73
COAL-FIRED POWER STATION · ELECTRICITY
DISTRIBUTION · NUCLEAR POWER STATION · STEAM
TURBINES · GENERATOR · HYDROELECTRIC POWER
STATION · TIDAL POWER STATION

COMMUNICATIONS

THE NEWSROOM 74–77
TELEPHONE · OPTICAL FIBER · MOBILE PHONE
BALLPOINT PEN · FAX MACHINE · COMPUTER
PRINTERS · BINOCULARS · SLR CAMERA

PRINTING A BOOK 78–81
TYPESETTER · COLOR SCANNER · PRINTING METHODS
COLOR PRINTING · PRINTING PRESS · PHOTOCOPIER

THE TELEVISION STUDIO 82–85
TELEPROMPTER · TELEVISION CAMERA · RHEOSTAT
ANIMATION · SATELLITE TELEVISION

Continued on next page

INTRODUCTION

Look around you. Unless you are reading this book on a desert island, or deep in the jungle, you should be able to see at least one kind of machine. It might be a very simple device, such as a pair of scissors, or a nut and bolt. Or it could be a complicated one, like a stereo music system, a car, or a jumbo jet flying overhead.

How does it work? Nearly all of us have a built-in curiosity about how things work – and especially about the workings of machines and bits of equipment designed by other humans. What happens inside the shiny white box of a dishwasher? Or in the great construction machines on a building site? Or even in an electric light bulb, when you flick on the switch?

How Things Work takes the lid off dozens of machines, devices, instruments, and pieces of equipment. Clear diagrams show how the parts move, and what goes where. It shows that many machines rely on basic mechanical and electrical parts, such as levers, screws, springs, and electromagnets. The trick is putting these simple parts together in the right way to do the job.

The book is divided into ten main sections, each based on a different aspect of our daily lives. See what happens when you wash your clothes or turn on the lawn sprinkler in *The Home*. Find out what oil rigs do and how electricity is made in *Power and Services*. And see how your own body works, and how plants and animals live together in nature, in *The Human Body* and *Wildlife and Farming*.

Many small devices, and the principles by which they work, are used again and again in different machines. These are explained in the *Glossary*, together with less familiar terms.

So, next time you pull on a new sweater, take the train to the next city, or watch a movie – think about the many processes and machines that have gone into making these things. They have been devised and constructed by people. Someone has to invent each machine, from a humble zipper to the printing press or the Space Shuttle. Great inventors started with their built-in curiosity and a desire to make things work. Could this be you?

GETTING UP

FLUORESCENT LIGHT 6

CLOCK 1

HAIR DRIER 4

TOILET TANK 5

FAUCET 3

AEROSOL SPRAY 8

ZIPPER 7

WARMTH AND WATER 2

1 **CLOCK**

The clock is one of the most familiar machines. In an escapement-type clock (as opposed to an electric one), energy for its mechanism comes from you, as you wind it up. The escape wheel clicks around slowly like a rotating ratchet, allowing the energy from the mainspring to unwind very slowly, and by regular amounts each time. The mechanism that measures out the small bursts of movement is the *escapement* mechanism. The energy from the mainspring keeps the balance wheel swinging back and forth. The pallets alternately catch and release the escape wheel. This breaks up the regular unwinding of the mainspring into small measured bursts of time which are then transmitted via the train of connecting gears to the minute and the hour hands.

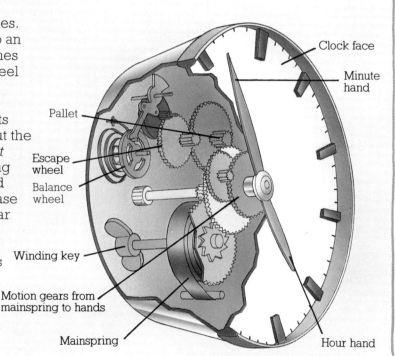

Clock face

Minute hand

Pallet

Escape wheel

Balance wheel

Winding key

Motion gears from mainspring to hands

Mainspring

Hour hand

WARMTH AND WATER

The walls and ceilings of most modern houses conceal a maze of water pipes. There are two major systems: one for the water supply itself, from taps, and a separate circuit for the central-heating system. Water from the water main flows under great pressure up into the roofspace, where it fills up the cold-water tank. Usually, one pipe runs from this incoming main to the kitchen cold-water faucet, which is why this tap has such a powerful flow if you turn it on full! Water from the cold-water tank flows to the cold taps in the bath, shower, and basin, and to the toilet tank (page 16).

BOILER

Expansion vent

Pressure relief valve

Insulated water tank

Hot water out

Cold water in

Drainage tap

Roofspace

Expansion tank

Cold-water tank

Room thermostat

Hot-water tank

Water main (supply)

Pump

Radiators

Cold water to cold taps

Hot water to hot taps

Hot water to radiators

Sink

No contact

Contact

Bimetal strip

Control dial

Strip bends this way when cool

The house's hot-water faucets are fed from the hot-water tank, which is kept full by water coming in from the cold-water tank when the level drops. The hot-water tank is heated by a separate system of hot water from the central-heating boiler. This circuit of water also flows through the radiators, to warm them. As water evaporates or leaks from the central-heating circuit, the hot-water tank is kept topped up from the cold-water tank. When the central-heating system switches on, the water in its circuits expands as it is heated. An expansion tank in the roofspace allows the water to increase in volume without bursting the pipes.

3 FAUCET

We rarely think of what happens inside a faucet until it starts to drip. As you turn the handle, the screw mechanism inside, which presses a rubber washer onto the water pipe, lifts up. The pressure of the water trying to push through the pipe pushes the washer upward, and so the water flows through. Water does not leak around the spindle because the spindle fits snugly inside the water-sealing nut. Newer faucets are made without washers.

Handle

Spindle

Handle is turned

Water flows out

Rubber washer

Water pressure

4 HAIR DRIER

The drier contains a miniature electric heater to create your own warm wind. The heating element is made from special resistance wire. This partially resists the flow of electricity through it, and heat is produced as the electricity forces its way through. The fan blows moisture-laden air away from your hair, continuously replacing it with fresh, dry air.

Cool air is sucked in

Fan

Heater elements

Air flows over heater elements

Warm air out

Nozzle

On-off switch

Bimetal cut-out in case of overheating

5 TOILET TANK

Many houses have several ballcocks, one in each flush tank. As water fills the tank, it lifts the large floating ball. Gradually the float arm attached to the ball closes a valve which stops the water. When you pull the handle, a large disk inside a bell lifts a quantity of water into the siphon tube. This water then falls down into the toilet bowl and pulls along the rest of the water by *siphonic action*. Eventually, the disk's edge wears and water leaks down past it when the handle is pulled. This is why a toilet tank gradually becomes more awkward to flush.

Float

Float arm

Pivot

Valve

Handle

Tank

Bowl

Siphon

Bell

To bowl

Lifting disk

Water inlet

Soil pipe

FLUSH

FILLING

FULL

6 FLUORESCENT LIGHT

A fluorescent striplight produces more light per amount of electricity than the light bulb (page 140). The tube is filled with vapor of the silvery metal mercury (found in thermometers, page 115). The metal electrode at the end of the tube gives off a beam of invisible, electrically charged particles, called electrons. When an electron hits a mercury atom, it momentarily knocks one of the atom's own electrons out of position. This creates a burst of ultraviolet light, which is turned into visible light by the tube's internal coating (page 131).

Free electrons pass along tube

Mercury vapor

Electrode

UV light makes tube coating glow

Glass tube

Phosphor coating

Electron

Mercury atom

Mercury electron knocked into high orbit

Falling electron emits UV light

SWITCH OFF

Rocker switch

Circuit broken

Circuit completed

SWITCH ON

7 ZIPPER

The classic zipper is made of two rows of alternating tooth-and-socket plates. These are opened and closed by wedges on the zipper pull, or slide. When you close the zipper, the teeth come together at an angle as they slide past the upper wedge. They are then clipped together by the lower wedges, with each tooth fitting into the socket of the one in front. The first zipper was invented by Whitcomb Judson in 1893.

Slide

Sockets

Teeth

Upper wedge

Lower wedges

Pressure pushes teeth into sockets

Teeth interlock

8 AEROSOL SPRAY

The contents of an aerosol can include the product itself and the propellant that carries it. They are under great pressure, and the outlet valve is kept closed both by this internal pressure and by a spring. As you push the button, the valve opens and allows the contents to flow. The outflow channel is very narrow and causes the product to break up into a fine, mistlike spray.

Spray channel

Spray

Button

Valve

Pressure-resistant casing

Spring

Feed tube

Propellant and product under pressure

THE KITCHEN

MICROWAVE OVEN 9

SCALES 4

REFRIGERATOR 10

ELECTRIC IRON 5

POP-UP TOASTER 2

ELECTRIC KETTLE 6

COFFEE PERCOLATOR 7

WASHING MACHINE 12

CLOTHES DRIER 13

DISHWASHER 11

CAN OPENER 1

EGGBEATER 3

FOOD PROCESSOR 8

CAN OPENER

The can opener is a good example of the wedge. Pull down the handle, and the cutter's sharp edge acts as a gradually widening wedge that forces its way into the lid. Turn the key, and the teeth on the wheel grip the rim and turn it around.

Handle lever

Handles are pulled together to drive cutter through lid

Turn key

Can

Circular cutter

Toothed wheels turn can around

POP-UP TOASTER

Making the morning toast relies on a simple electrical device, the bimetallic strip. This is found in temperature controls of many kinds. It is made of two metal strips joined side by side. One metal expands faster with heat than the other. As the bimetallic strip warms up, due to heat around it or electricity passing through it, one side expands and lengthens faster than the other. The strip arches into a curve. Its end eventually touches a metal contact, to complete an electric circuit – in this case, for an *electromagnet*.

Heater elements

Bread

Browning control

Bimetallic strip

Spring

Electromagnet

Bimetallic strip makes contact and switches on electromagnet

Catch is released

Electromagnet attracts hinge

EGGBEATER

It is hard to imagine a simpler example of gearing than the kitchen eggbeater. Turn the large double-sided gearwheel slowly. The smaller gearwheels have fewer teeth, so they rotate faster. Count their rotations for one turn of the handle – this is the gearing ratio.

Double-sided large gearwheel

Small driven gearwheels

Beaters turn in opposite directions

Handle

SCALES

Spring-balance scales are based on the fact that increasing weights stretch an attached spring longer and longer. This movement is converted from linear (straight) to rotary (circular) using the rack, which is a "straightened" gearwheel. It turns a pinion (round gearwheel) attached to the pointer.

Spring pulls rack upward

Dial

Toothed rack moves up

Weight pushes lever down

Pinion moves around

5 **ELECTRIC IRON**

Old-fashioned "smoothing irons" were warmed on a stand near the fire or hotplate. Today's electric version has its own heater element that warms the soleplate. Most materials press more smoothly if they are damp, since moisture softens the tiny fibers in the material and makes them flexible. So the "steam iron" sprays steam or a fine mist of hot water onto the material.

Steam button and control
Water filler
Water tank
Drip valve
Steam chamber
Filter
Soleplate

6 **ELECTRIC KETTLE**

Like the iron, the modern kettle has its own electrical heater element. It also contains two failsafe circuit-breakers, or cut-outs. One stops the electric current to the heater when the water reaches boiling point. The other does the same if the kettle boils dry. The plug and socket must be designed so that water cannot drip into them and cause a short-circuit.

Water level guide
On-off switch
Drip-protected plug and socket
Heater element

7 **COFFEE PERCOLATOR**

In a coffee grinder, beans slide down between two ridged metal surfaces that fit closely together. The turning motion of the handle crushes the beans into a powder fine enough to fall into the tray below. The percolator uses the principle that hot water gives off air bubbles and rises. The bubbles and hot water stream up the central spout, to create a fountain at the top. The hot water percolates, or trickles, back down through the ground coffee, dissolving the coffee-flavored substances as it goes.

GRINDER
Turn handle
Coffee beans
Ground coffee powder collects in tray
Beans crushed by metal ridges

PERCOLATOR
Cone collects hot water and air bubbles from base
Spout
Ground coffee
Water percolates (trickles) through coffee
Heat

FOOD PROCESSOR

The food processor is another kitchen device that uses electrical power instead of muscle power. Inside, the typical processor is relatively simple. An electric motor turns the spindle via a flexible toothed belt. Each differently shaped attachment does a specific job, from slicing to shredding to beating to liquefying. Ingredients are dropped into the feed tube, or pushed in using a plunger. This keeps fingers away from the whirling blades; safe design is a vital feature of many machines.

Controls

Electric motor

Attachment slots onto splines (ridges) on spindle

Feed tube

Lid

Toothed belt

Spindle

MICROWAVE OVEN

Microwaves are part of the spectrum of *electromagnetic waves*, which include light waves and X-rays. Microwaves have wavelengths from about 12 inches to .004 inch, which places them between the shortest radio waves and infrared (heat) waves. One of their properties is to excite molecules, especially in liquids, and make them vibrate and heat up. So foods with a large proportion of water, such as soups, cook quickest.

The waves are produced by a *magnetron*, a type of electron tube. They are scattered around the oven by a metal fan, for more even cooking. They pass through most types of china and glass, but not metals.

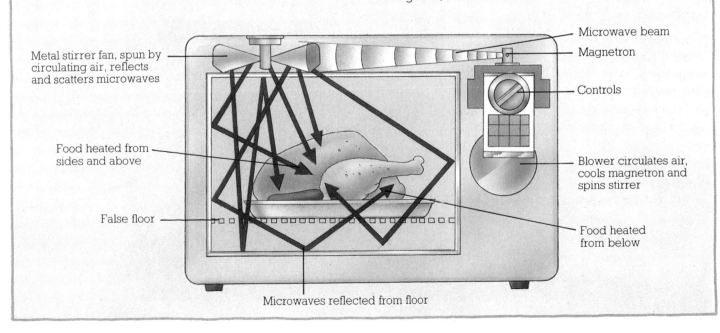

Metal stirrer fan, spun by circulating air, reflects and scatters microwaves

Microwave beam

Magnetron

Controls

Food heated from sides and above

Blower circulates air, cools magnetron and spins stirrer

False floor

Food heated from below

Microwaves reflected from floor

10 REFRIGERATOR

The refrigerator does not make coldness out of nothing. It works as a heat exchanger, extracting warmth from the air inside the unit and passing it into the air outside. The coolant is a special pressurized fluid that flows around a circuit, from evaporator to condenser. In the evaporator, inside the unit, the coolant boils under relatively high pressure. Being a boiling liquid, it draws heat from its surroundings. (In fact, the coolant's boiling point is lower than water's freezing point.) It then flows under even higher pressure to the condenser. Here it turns from a gas back into a liquid and gives out heat to the air as it does so.

Condenser (warmest)
Evaporator (coldest)
Insulated casing
Thermostat
Radiator vanes give off heat
Very thin (capillary) tube causes pressure to build up before coolant reaches condenser
Filter/drier cleans coolant and collects moisture
Compressor pressurizes coolant

11 DISHWASHER

Dirty dishes and silverware are loaded into specially designed carriers, so that the water spray can reach all parts and the water can drain away freely afterward. The pressure of the water itself makes the jets spin around. The first part of the cycle uses water containing detergent, to dissolve grease and grime. The detergent is loaded into a compartment in the lid. In the second part of the cycle, clean water rinses away the soapy water. Then a heating element warms and dries the load.

Water outlet
Water inlet
Rotating spray jets
Water softener
Collecting tray in base
Detergent compartment
Heater element
Drain
Pump
Filter
PATTERN OF WATER JETS

12 WASHING MACHINE

A modern washing machine relies on several regulatory mechanisms in its operation. At the start of the cycle, water pours into the drum through an electrically controlled inlet valve. Once the water reaches a certain level in the drum, a sensor turns off the inlet valve. The pressure of the water in the inlet pipe helps to shut the valve firmly. The water is then heated by the machine's heater element. Once the pre-set temperature is reached, a *thermostat* switches off the electricity supply to the heater. A load of washing and water is very heavy, so the drum is stabilized by weights and suspended by heavy-duty springs.

Rotating drum

Inlet valve

Water runs through detergent compartment into drum

Controls

Heater element

Filter

Drain pump

Main motor

Water outlet

Suspension springs

13 CLOTHES DRIER

In most tumble driers, the electric motor is programmed to turn the drum one way and then go into reverse and spin it the other way. This helps to shake and separate the contents. It prevents them from clumping together and leaving a still-damp patch in the middle, which the drying air cannot reach. Hot air is drawn through the unit by a blower fan. As it passes through the load, the air picks up dust and fibers; these are trapped by the filter screen. In order to heat such great volumes of air, clothes driers use lots of electricity. They have one of the highest running costs of all household machines.

Drum rotates in alternate directions

Casing

Air passes through load

Heater elements

Timer

Door

Filter screen

Air blown out

Blower

Drive belt

Air sucked in

THE GARDEN

ELECTRIC DRILL

CHAINSAW

SCREWDRIVER

WHEELBARROW

GARDEN SHEARS

GREENHOUSE

LAWNMOWER

LAWN SPRINKLER

1

GREENHOUSE

Glass lets light rays pass through easily but lets heat (infrared) pass less easily. The sun's light can pass easily into the greenhouse, but its heat cannot. However, inside the greenhouse, some of the sun's light rays are absorbed by the objects and converted into heat – which cannot get out again easily. The heat is trapped and gradually builds up. This type of warming is called the greenhouse effect. Many scientists believe it will warm the whole earth in coming years.

Sun's rays converted to heat (infrared) inside greenhouse

Sun's light and heat

Ultraviolet light reflected by glass

Glass traps heat inside, warming air in greenhouse

SCREWDRIVER

The screwdriver acts like a lever. Your hand moves in a large circle as you turn the handle. The turning force, or torque, is transmitted down the shaft and blade, into the screw head's slot. The screw turns in a smaller circle, but with greater turning power. Slot-headed screws are for general work. Cross-headed screws are less likely to let the blade slip out and damage the nearby surface.

Small force turning large distance

Handle

Shaft

Head

Large force turning small distance

Screw acts as a spiral ramp

LAWNMOWER

Like the screwdriver, the lawnmower is a rotary machine. In the hand-pushed type, the heavy back roller is linked to the rotating blades by a chain. The rotating blades are angled in the form of a shallow helix, so that each one approaches the base blade with a scissorlike action. Grass is trapped between the two, snipped off, and thrown into the grass box.

The height of the cut is adjusted by lowering or raising the small front roller. In a power mower, a small gasoline engine drives the back roller and blades.

Handle

Front roller

Rotating blades

Base blade

Back roller

Grass box

Rotating blade and base blade come together with scissor action

Toothed wheel turns rotating blades

Cut grass

Front roller

Mower moves forward

Uncut grass

4 LAWN SPRINKLER

The oscillating sprinkler is based on the principle of the water wheel. The pressure of the water coming through the hosepipe turns a small fan-shaped water wheel, just as running water turns turbines in a giant hydroelectric power station (page 72). A series of gears slows down the spinning speed, and a crank fixed to a rotating wheel changes the circular motion to an oscillating one (swinging back and forth like a pendulum). By changing the length of the crank, the sprayer can be made to cover a wide or narrow area on either side.

Spray tube

Water flows into spray tube

Water flow turns water wheel

Crank changes rotary (turning) motion into oscillating (back-and-forth) motion

Hosepipe

Base

Gearing slows down turning motion

Water wheel spins series of gears

5 CHAINSAW

In a hand saw, the teeth oscillate (move back and forth). The chainsaw has a ''never-ending'' blade, in the shape of a chain loop bearing teeth. A small engine, usually gasoline-driven, turns the drive cog and makes the chain move around its loop. The chain soon becomes hot and tends to stick in its guides. For cooling and lubrication, oil is regularly dripped onto it from a small tank. Safety is vital. Users wear strong gloves, protective goggles, shin-guards, and thick boots, in case the cutting chain slips and falls.

Chain guard

Chain guide

Small internal-combustion engine

Handle

Pull starter

Drive cog

Chain carries cutting teeth

Tip sprocket

6 ELECTRIC DRILL

The small electric motor in a drill is extremely powerful, and its turning force is increased as it is slowed down by the gearing mechanism. In many drills, speeds are adjustable either by varying the electrical voltage fed to the motor or by changing the gears. Speeds of only a few hundred rpm (revolutions per minute) are suitable for tough materials such as concrete and hard metal. Several thousand rpm can be used in softer materials such as softwoods and plastics.

Electric motor

Cooling fan

Gearing mechanism

Drive shaft

Adjustable chuck for different sized drill bits

Drill bit

Handle

Speed trigger

Bit rotates

Waste runs up spiral grooves and out of hole

Tip of bit

7 WHEELBARROW

The wheelbarrow is one of the simplest examples of a lever. The pivot point, or fulcrum, is at one end. Using a wheelbarrow, you can lift a large weight over a small distance by applying your small lifting effort over a large distance.

Effort moves greater distance

Fulcrum at wheel

Load moves small distance

8 GARDEN SHEARS

Two levers connected together give the shears plenty of cutting power. Shearing pressure is greatest near the fulcrum. The blades should be sharp and come together without gaps or twisting.

Handle moves large distance with little force

Blade moves small distance with great force

Fulcrum at bolt-and-nut pivot

THE STREET

PADLOCK 5

PUMPS AND VALVES 4

DUMP TRUCK 8

TRAFFIC SIGNALS 7

COMBINATION LOCK 6

BRAKES 3

GEARS 2

BALANCING 1

JACKHAMMER 9

1 BALANCING

A spinning wheel acts as a simple gyroscope (page 45). It resists attempts to change position. Hold a rotating wheel as shown, and feel the resistance as you try to tip it. This *gyroscopic inertia* helps you to balance on a bicycle.

2 GEARS

Pedaling downhill, the bicycle chain runs from the large front sprocket to the small rear one. For every turn of the pedals, the road wheel turns many times, but with limited turning force. Uphill, the chain runs from the

Chain

Four sprockets

Gear lever mechanism

Gear changing mechanism

BRAKES

Brakes do not press on the bicycle tire – they would soon wear a hole in it! They press on the wheel rim. The two metal arms, or yokes, work as levers. They close the blocks onto the rim with a scissor action, for even pressure on each side. Use the rear brake for routine braking, and both brakes in an emergency. Do not pull hard on the front brake alone. You could fly over the handlebars.

BRAKES OFF   BRAKES ON

Cable

Yoke   Pivot

Spring

Brake shoe

Tire

PUMPS AND VALVES

These are components of many machines, from faucets to jet planes. The pump applies pressure to a fluid (gas or liquid), for example, by a piston (page 88). This makes the fluid flow to a region of lower pressure. Non-return valve designs are many and varied, but their main job is to allow fluid to flow one way but not the other. Some valves use hinged doors, others have flexible diaphragms or lever-operated closures.

Handle

Plunger

Valve

AIR IN   AIR OUT

Hose

Inner tube

Valve

Tire

AIR IN   AIR OUT

small front sprocket to the large rear one. The road wheel turns more slowly but with greater force. Racing cyclists use gears to keep up their natural rate of pedaling whether going uphill or down.

HARDER TO PEDAL
FASTER SPEED

EASIER TO PEDAL
SLOWER SPEED

5 PADLOCK

This small security device has the same basic mechanism as a door lock or a car ignition. Grooves and ridges run lengthwise along the key, and the keyhole is shaped to accept only keys of a certain shape. When inserted, the key's V-cuts push small locking pins into exact alignment (a straight line), which permits the locking cylinder (barrel) to turn. A lever at its end drags back the locking bolt, thereby freeing the lock.

Shackle

Locking bolt

Locking cylinder

Locking pin

WRONG KEY

CORRECT KEY

6 COMBINATION LOCK

Like the padlock, the combination lock relies on alignment. In this case, only when the tumblers are turned to the correct number combination do the slots inside them line up. This lets you withdraw the key. With four number tumblers, and the numbers 0–9 on each one, how many possible number combinations are there? (Answer on page 151).

Spaces

Key

CORRECT NUMBERS

SCRAMBLED NUMBERS

7 TRAFFIC SIGNALS

Older-type signals run to a preset timed cycle. If a car pulls up just as they change from green to red, it has to wait for the cycle to be completed before the lights will change to green again. Newer-style signals respond to a car's presence. The car's metal parts interfere with a weak magnetic field set up by the electrical wire buried in the road. The control box senses this and, if there are no cars waiting to move in the other directions, it switches the signals to green.

CAR INTERFERES WITH MAGNETIC FIELD

Signal

Control box

Magnetic field

Loop in road

8 DUMP TRUCK

A dump truck has a powerful hydraulic system enabling it to lift heavy loads. The power for the system is taken from the truck's diesel engine via gearing and a control box. A hydraulic arm pushes a lever, called the lifting arm, supplying the force to lift the truck body. The body moves in an arc as it is unloaded or loaded. If the tipping hooks are raised, they grab the base of the body and tip it, and the dump truck dumps.

LOADING

UNLOADING

Lifting arm

Body

Tipping hook

Control box

9 JACKHAMMER

Unlike the rotary electric drill (page 27), the jackhammer is pneumatic and percussive. "Pneumatic" means that it is driven by compressed air (page 36). This is important for safety, since it means there are no trailing electrical wires. "Percussive" refers to hitting. The jackhammer breaks into the road surface using a fast series of hammer blows. These are produced by a flip-flop diaphragm valve which reroutes the air many times each second, alternately raising and lowering the piston.

Control lever

Valve

Air outlet

Diaphragm

Cylinder

Air inlet

Piston

Anvil

UPSTROKE

DOWNSTROKE

TAKING TO THE TRACKS

STEAM LOCOMOTIVE 1

DIESEL LOCOMOTIVE 2

DIESEL-ELECTRIC LOCOMOTIVE 3

RAIL NETWORK 7

SIGNALS 6

BUFFERS 5

ELECTRIC LOCOMOTIVE 4

Steam in
Steam out
Steam in
Steam out

1

STEAM LOCOMOTIVE
During the first half of the 18th century, British engineers such as Thomas Savery, John Newcomen, and James Watt developed the steam engine. As water is heated, it boils into steam, which takes up far more space. This expansion from a liquid to a gas provides the pressure which pushes the pistons along inside the cylinders of the steam locomotive. But the steam locomotive is inefficient: much of the energy in its fuel, coal, is wasted as heat.

Chimney Smoke box

Boiler Regulator

Firebox

Fire doors

Piston

Flywheel

2 DIESEL LOCOMOTIVE

The sources of power for this locomotive are diesel engines (page 89). The diesel engine was invented in the 1890s by the French-born German engineer Rudolf Diesel. Diesel engines are more efficient than steam ones: their fuel contains more energy per weight than coal, and their maintenance time and running costs are lower. Immense force is transmitted to the driving wheel through a hydraulic gearing system. The most powerful steam locomotives, American "Big Boys," produced 7,000 horsepower (about 5.25 million watts). Diesel locomotives are capable of similar feats.

Diesel engine

Cooling system

Hydraulic system   Fuel tanks   Gearbox

3 DIESEL-ELECTRIC LOCOMOTIVE

This traction (pulling) unit is in effect an electric locomotive with its own source of electricity. The diesel engine turns a large generator, which produces electricity to drive electric motors. There is usually one electric motor on each axle. The motors are efficient and flexible; they produce high turning force even at low speeds. This means that there is no need for an expensive and energy-wasting gear system. Union Pacific Railroad's turbocharged diesel-electric locomotives are the most powerful, producing 6,600 horsepower (about 4.95 million watts).

Diesel engine

Generator

Engineer's cab

Electric motor

Fuel tanks   Battery compartment

4 ELECTRIC LOCOMOTIVE

The electric locomotive picks up electricity at 25,000 volts AC (alternating current) from overhead or trackside power lines with a pantograph. The current is converted into DC (direct current) by *rectifiers* and *transformers*, and fed via motor control circuits to the drive motors. These are mounted in the locomotive, or "power car," and they drive the wheels through a series of gears. The main disadvantage of this system is the high cost of building and maintaining the overhead power lines, and the fact that the train cannot go where there are no power lines.

High-voltage overhead power lines

Pantograph

Motor control circuits

Automatic control panel

Voltage control circuits

Drive motors

Storage batteries

Air conditioning unit

Engineer's cab

5 BUFFERS

Stationary buffers are mounted at the end of a railway line. Buffers are also fitted to locomotives, passenger cars and freight cars. The metal spring and hydraulic damping fluid absorb the energy of the moving vehicle, causing it to slow down gradually without shocks or jarring.

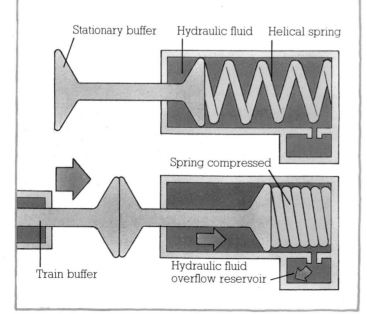

Stationary buffer   Hydraulic fluid   Helical spring

Spring compressed

Train buffer

Hydraulic fluid overflow reservoir

6 SIGNALS

Each rail network has its own signal design. The basic function of the signals is to inform the engineer that the line is clear or to warn that it is not. The four-aspect system gives plenty of time for the engineer to slow the train so that passengers are not jerked by a sudden halt.

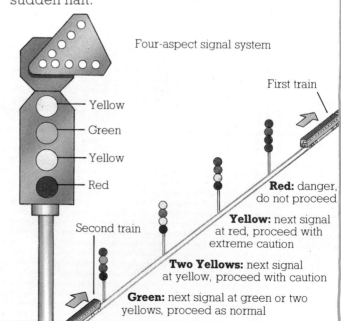

Four-aspect signal system

First train

Yellow

Green

Yellow

Red

Second train

Red: danger, do not proceed

Yellow: next signal at red, proceed with extreme caution

Two Yellows: next signal at yellow, proceed with caution

Green: next signal at green or two yellows, proceed as normal

RAIL NETWORK

Today's railway system is a complicated maze of tracks, switches, signals, crossings, passenger stations, and freight yards. Most trains cannot climb steep gradients, so the tracks have to be made relatively level by cutting through hills and building embankments in valleys. The main signal boxes are the nerve centers of the network, controlling the signals and the switches. They can divert a slower freight train to allow through a passenger express, or switch a commuter train onto a local line for suburban stations.

There are approximately 273,400 miles of track in North America, 60,900 in South America, 261,000 in Europe, 90,100 in Asia, and 46,600 in Africa. The world's longest railway line runs across the USSR from Moscow to the Soviet east coast, a distance of almost 5,900 miles with a journey time of more than eight days.

PANTOGRAPH SYSTEM

Overhead line
Collector pan
Pantograph arms
Spring
Piston

Overhead line

Bridge

Level crossing for road traffic

Signal box

Embankment

Cutting

SWITCHING

Gap

Switches swing to right

Rail touches

Sidings

Buffers

SLEEPER RAIL-SUPPORT SYSTEM

Railclip

Steel rail

Wooden or concrete sleeper

THIRD-RAIL SYSTEM

Third rail carries electricity

Pick-up shoe connects to motor

Insulator below third rail

THE HIGHWAY

GAS PUMP 2

PNEUMATIC TIRE 5

REFLECTORS 4

MAKING A HIGHWAY 6

AIR COMPRESSOR 1

HYDRAULIC JACK 3

WRENCH AND NUT 3

---

1 ### AIR COMPRESSOR

The piston-based air compressor produces air at high pressure. This is used to operate machines such as the jackhammer (page 31) or the compressed-air nut-remover. It is also used to inflate pneumatic tires (page 39). Air is pulled in above the piston, pushed around the bypass to below the piston, and then compressed and forced out as more air is pulled in above the piston. The piston is driven by an electric motor or internal combustion engine.

Air transferred to below piston

Valve closed

Valve open

Valve closed

Valve open

Piston moves up

Valve open

Fresh air sucked in

Valve closed

Compressed air blown out

Valve open

Valve closed

Piston moves down

2 GAS PUMP

There are several main mechanisms within a gas pump. One is the motor-driven pump itself, which draws up fuel from the large underground storage tank. Next is the filter to remove dirt and impurities. An air separator draws off bubbles of air and other gases. Then comes the meter that measures the volume, or quantity, of fuel passing through and shows the amount on the dial or display. Finally, there is the hose and nozzle. There is often a detector in the hose, warning that the fuel tank of the vehicle is getting full.

Register dials or display
Volume meter
Air vent and flame trap
Fumes vent
Float
Air separator
Filter
Rotary pump
Pump motor
Sight glass to check for air bubbles
Valve
Hose nozzle
Inlet pipe from underground storage tank

3 HYDRAULIC JACK

The vehicle jack converts a small force that pushes a long way into a large force that pushes a short way. The jack's handle moves a small piston a significant distance. This creates pressure in the hydraulic fluid, which presses on a secondary, or slave, piston. The slave piston has a much larger area, so it moves a short way but with greater total force. When the handle is pumped repeatedly, the jack gradually rises.

Fluid slowly forces slave piston up
Pumping handle
Large slave piston
Fluid reservoir
Small action piston
Valves
Fluid pumped into slave cylinder

WRENCH AND NUT

The wrench's action is based on the lever principle: a small force moving a greater distance is converted into a greater force moving a small distance. The flat sides on the nut should fit snugly inside the corresponding slots in a wrench.

Handle moves long distance with little turning force
Hexagonal bolt
Wrench acts as a lever
Head moves short distance with great turning force
Nut

4 REFLECTORS

Driving in the dark would be much more difficult without road reflectors to define the lane markings. The reflector contains a curved mirror and a half-spherical lens (page 77). When a light is shone on the reflector, the mirror and lens combine to focus and reflect the light rays back out, in the opposite direction. The device is sometimes called a cat's eye because the eyes of a cat contain a special reflecting layer, the tapetum, so that they too glow in the dark when a light is shone onto them.

Rubber pad contains two reflectors

Mirrored rear surface of lens

Center of curvature of mirror and lens

Spherical lens

Incoming and reflected light path

Cast-iron base set into road surface

6 MAKING A HIGHWAY

The road surface may not look very interesting as you speed along in a car, a few feet above it. But road surfaces are the subject of constant research and improvement. They must have a combination of good strength, resistance to wear and to extremes of temperature and frost, excellent grip for tires in dry and wet conditions, and a certain amount of flexibility so that they do not crack and flake. The main types of road surface today are based on asphaltic concrete, which is a mix of asphalt, gravel, sand, and concrete. The surface has a "camber," that is, a slight arched or domed shape in the center, so that water drains off the sides.

Concrete mixer delivers load

Vibrator settles concrete and removes air pockets

Spreader distributes even layer of concrete

Granular sub-base

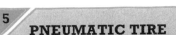

PNEUMATIC TIRE

Unlike a liquid, a gas can be compressed. It stores the energy used to compress it and releases this energy as a rebound when the pressure eases. The air-filled pneumatic tire works on this basis. The pressurized air inside the tire carries nine-tenths of the load, and the flexible walls of the tire carry the rest. The pressure of the air inside the tire presses the bead, or inner edge, onto the wheel rim for an airtight fit. The first practical pneumatic tires were invented by John Dunlop in 1888.

RADIAL
Belts at varying angles
Radials
Tread
Ribs
Sidewall
Rim flange
Chafer
Bead wires
Filler

CROSS-PLY
Belts at opposing angles
Tread
Ribs
Side-wall
Rim flange
Chafer
Ply cuffs
Bead wires
Filler

Strengthening steel meshwork laid over plastic sheet

Second concrete layer smoothed and settled

Topmost layer of concrete with roughened surface for good tire grip

Heavy-duty plastic sheet laid over concrete

The tarmacadam surface is crushed stone in a mixture of tar, bitumen, and asphalt. Tarmacadam is named after the nineteenth-century Scottish engineer John McAdam.

Crash barrier
White lane markings
Reflectors
Layers of tarmacadam
Concrete base
Drains and other services
Granular sub-base

THE DOCKS

MAGNETIC COMPASS
3

SUBMARINE
6

MANEUVERIN

PROPELLER
1
2

ANEMOMETER
4

RO-RO FERRY
5

HOVERCRAFT
7

HYDROFOIL
8

Angled screw blades

Water forced past blades

Direction of spin

1

PROPELLER
The propeller is also called a screw. As it spins, it pulls water past it. Water is naturally viscous, which means that it is sticky and does not flow easily. It therefore resists the motion of the propeller, and so the propeller, and the craft attached to it, are pushed forward. The propeller of an aircraft is similar. It has longer and thinner blades because air is much less viscous than water. The largest ship's screw is 36 feet in diameter.

2 MANEUVERING

Ships, planes, and similar craft that move through fluids change direction by using control surfaces (page 46). The rudder is the control surface for steering to the left or right. If the rudder is angled into the flow of water (or air) past it, the moving water (or air) pushes against it (the action). To obey the first law of motion there is a reaction, which pushes the control surface back and tries to make it parallel with the flow of the water or air. As the rudder swings around, so does the craft attached to it.

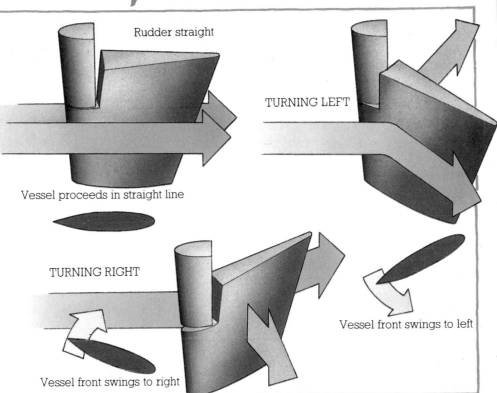

Rudder straight

Vessel proceeds in straight line

TURNING LEFT

TURNING RIGHT

Vessel front swings to right

Vessel front swings to left

3 MAGNETIC COMPASS

If a magnetized object is left to hang freely, the earth's weak magnetic field acts on it, to make the object line up with the earth's own lines of force. As only unlike poles of a magnet attract each other, it is the south pole of a magnetic compass that is pulled toward the earth's own North Pole. A ship's compass floats on oil in order to remain steady in high seas.

Scale marked in degrees of the compass

Points of magnetic compass

Magnet

Oil

Gimbals keep compass level even in rough seas

4 ANEMOMETER

Sailors need to know the wind speed, to calculate how far they are being blown off course, to warn of approaching storms, or to help them decide which sails to set. The anemometer's cups are spun by the wind. The faster they spin, the more electricity is produced in the small generator, and the higher is the dial or display reading.

Revolving cups

Direction of spin

Central shaft

Low wind speed, low current generated

High wind speed, high current generated

Generator

Electrical current to wind speed display

5 RO-RO FERRY

The word *ro-ro* (Roll-On-Roll-Off) refers to the way that vehicles can drive in one end of the ferry along a ramp and drive off a ramp at the other end without being lifted by a crane or having to turn around inside. The ferry has propellers at both bow and stern (front and back), and often along the sides too, so that it can maneuver forward, backward, and sideways. The heaviest vehicles are usually put on the ferry's lower decks. This gives the ferry a lower center of gravity, which means that it has greater stability and is tossed around less in rough weather.

Vehicle decks

Restaurant

Rear loading doors

Rear propellers

Stabilizers

Engine ro[...]

6 SUBMARINE

Curved surfaces resist pressure better than flat ones (as in the aerosol can, page 17, and the bridge arch, page 56). The submarine can withstand great pressures as it dives beneath the waves. Sonar (SOund NAvigation and Ranging) enables the submarine to navigate and detect objects under water. High-pitched "pings" of sound are given off by the transmitter, and a series of hydrophones (underwater microphones) listens for the returning echoes. From the direction of the echoes, and the time they take to return, computers on board the submarine can calculate an object's direction, its distance or ranging, its size and shape. In passive sonar, the submarine simply listens for noises produced by other craft.

Radar masts and periscopes

Conning tower

Control room

Passive sonar: sub simply listens

Escape hatch

Nuclear reactor

Active sonar: sub sends out sonar pings and listens for their echoes

Crew deck

Front hydroplane

Sonar in bow

Bridge

Front loading doors

Lifeboats

Front propellers

7 HOVERCRAFT

By skimming over waves rather than through them, the hovercraft has several advantages over a normal ship. It can ride small waves more quickly and smoothly, and it can "fly" straight up a ramp from water onto land.

The hovercraft is raised by downward air currents blown from large lifting fans. The air currents are partly trapped within the flexible enclosing skirt. This produces the increased air pressure that forces the vehicle upward.

Turbine engines

Forward propellers

Lifting fan

Gearbox

Lifting fan

Flexible skirt

Lift airstream

8 HYDROFOIL

The foil of the hydrofoil is shaped like an aircraft wing. As in a helicopter rotor blade (page 67), it converts forward motion into lift, and this raises the hull (the body of the vehicle) out of the water. Since the hull is clear of the water, the drag effect of the water (the force that slows things

down) is removed. Hydrofoil ferries travel at up to 50 knots (56 miles per hour) and carry over 200 passengers.

Ultrasonic sensors detect the height and speed of the craft and the oncoming wave pattern, and tilt or adjust the foils as necessary to stay stable.

Gearboxes

Rudder

Propeller

Rear hydroplane

Slow speed, hull sits in water

Fast speed, hydrofoil lifts hull clear of water

Cross-section of hydrofoil

Lift

Curved upper surface

Low water pressure over upper surface at speed creates lift

ON AN AIRLINER

JUMBO JET
4

FLIGHT DECK
2

RADIO AND RADAR
1

LIFEJACKET
3

1 RADIO AND RADAR

Aircraft use radio in two ways for navigation. In radar (RAdio Detection And Ranging), the aircraft's transmitter sends out bursts of radio signals. These bounce off the ground and objects such as buildings and other aircraft. The aircraft detects the returning echoes with its receiver (the principle is the same as for sonar, page 42). Radar equipment is usually hoisted in the radome, in the aircraft's nose (page 46). In addition, ground stations send out radio signals. (Each station has a different code.) The receiver picks up these signals, and from their direction and strength, the flight-deck computers can pinpoint the plane's position.

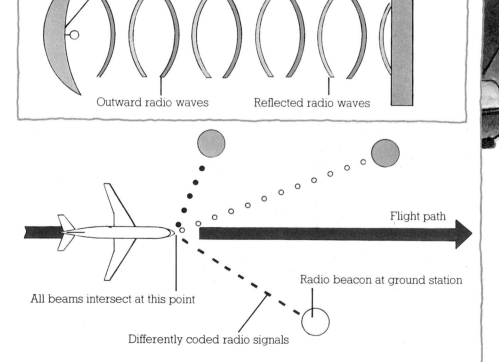

RADAR   Transmitter/receiver   Reflective surface

Outward radio waves   Reflected radio waves

Flight path

All beams intersect at this point

Radio beacon at ground station

Differently coded radio signals

2 FLIGHT DECK

The flight deck of a modern jetliner has dozens of displays and controls. These are carefully designed and positioned so that the crew can concentrate on the most important ones; they notice the others only if a problem arises. The airspeed indicator shows the aircraft's speed through the air. The altimeter, which uses the same principle as a *barometer*, measures height above sea level. A *gyroscope* is linked to the "attitude display," which shows whether the aircraft is flying level or tilted to one side.

Airspeed indicator

Altimeter

Pitot tube   Pressure sensor

AIRSTREAM

Air pressure builds up

Hairspring

Rocking bar   Arm

Pressure change with altitude alters size of near-vacuum capsule

Airspeed indicator
Artificial horizon
Altimeter

Control column

Foot pedals

Thrust controls for engines

Attitude display
Artificial horizon
Aircraft symbol
Roll movements of aircraft
Three-gimbaled gyroscope

Gyroscope stays steady

3 LIFEJACKET

Airliners carry lifejackets, and instructions to show passengers how to use them, for all journeys over water. Some jackets are blown up by the wearer. Others self-inflate when a cord is pulled. When the jacket enters sea water, a chemical reaction causes a light to flash. This signals to rescuers the position of the person needing help.

Air blown through

Light

Pea rolls around

Sound waves produced

Whistle

Saltwater detector

JUMBO JET

One of the most complex machines in the world, the airliner consists of several million separate parts – from turbine blades in the jet engines to passenger headphones for the movie soundtrack. The separate parts are grouped into a series of systems. The parts within each system work together to perform one overall function. The compressors, pistons and pressurized fluid in the hydraulic pipes, which work the various control surfaces and landing gear, make up the *hydraulic system*. The hundreds of miles of wiring, which connect different parts all over the aircraft to the flight-deck controls and displays, make up the *electrical system*. The fuel tanks, pumps, and pipes comprise the *fuel system*. The structural parts, such as the fuselage, wings, tailplane, and fin, make up the *airframe*.

Cruising at 600 miles per hour, 30,000 feet up, an airliner's wing provides lift, like a helicopter's rotor (page 67). When the plane takes off or comes in to land, various parts of its wing lift away. The shape of the wing as seen from the side – called the airfoil section – changes, according to the speed of the aircraft. Spoilers at the front of the wing interrupt the airflow over the front, or leading edge, while flaps at the back give extra lift at slower speeds.

Inboard spoiler

Outboard spoiler

Outboard aileron

Outboard flap

Inboard flap

Lounge

Flight deck

Forward cabin

Radar in nose cone

Nose landing gear

Door

Fuel tank

An aircraft moving in three dimensions – up/down, left/right, forward/backward – does so by changing its position on three axes, as shown below: pitch, yaw and spin, or roll. Passenger jets can make quite sharp turns and sudden dives, but they do not normally carry out such aerobatics.

ROLL

PITCH

YAW

Rudder

Tailplane

Elevator

Fin

Fuselage

Emergency exit

Rear cabin

Galley

INCREASED LIFT

This quiet, efficient jet engine swallows one ton of air each second. The air is compressed, mixed with fuel, and burned in the combustion chamber. Hot gases blast out of the back, and the engine reacts by being pushed forward. The large turbofan at the front blows some of the air around the main engine, to cool and quiet it and to give extra thrust.

Trailing edge

Wing   Spoiler

Fan   Central shaft   Compressor turbine blades

Leading edge

Engine mounting pylon

AIR INTAKE

Exhaust

Combustion chamber

Turbofan jet engine

INTO SPACE

SOLID-FUEL BOOSTER 3

SATELLITE 1

ROCKET 2

SPACE SHUTTLE 4

NASA

1 SATELLITE

A satellite does not need to be streamlined in order to fly through space, since there is no air in space to slow it down. But it does need a source of energy for its electronic circuitry. Sunlight is very strong in space, so the satellite has large solar panels that turn sunlight into electricity. A satellite must stay in exactly the right position, with its dish antennae facing the radio stations on the ground. For this reason, it is equipped with small gas thrusters which can tilt and twist the satellite into the correct orbit high above Earth.

Thrusters

Solar panels

Reaction wheels

Fuel tanks

SUNLIGHT

Negative terminal

Light causes electrons to move through layers, creating electric current

Positive terminal

2 ROCKET

A spacecraft must reach a speed of 25,000 miles per hour before it can break free of Earth's gravity and head into space. This is called the escape velocity. One huge rocket engine would make the spacecraft too heavy. The multistage launcher is designed to leave its engines and empty fuel tanks behind, stage by stage. As it climbs, smaller engines are sufficient to overcome the weakening pull of Earth's gravity. Nothing can burn without oxygen. Rocket fuel cannot therefore burn on its own in space, since there is no oxygen (or any other gas). So the rocket takes its own supply, an oxidizer in supercooled liquid form. The fuel and the oxidizer react in the combustion chamber (*see below*), in a kind of slow, controlled explosion.

Satellites folded into cargo bay

Third stage

Nose fairings

Second stage

First stage

Solid-fuel boosters

Fuel

Low pressure pumps

Oxidizer

Preburners

High pressure fuel pump

Hot gas

Hot gas

High pressure oxidizer pump

Heat exchanger

Combustion chamber

3 SOLID-FUEL BOOSTER

Instead of supercooled fuel in liquid form, the solid-fuel booster has fuel "cake" made of aluminum perchlorate, iron oxide, binders and curing chemicals. Once ignited, the booster fires steadily, but its burn cannot be altered or switched off. It boosts acceleration at the start of the launch. The launcher *Ariane*'s boosters burn out and fall away 42 seconds after lift-off.

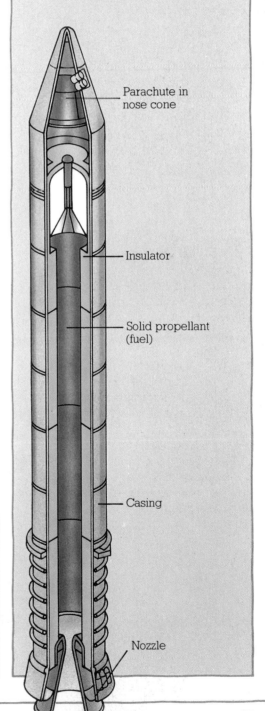

Parachute in nose cone

Insulator

Solid propellant (fuel)

Casing

Nozzle

Astronauts outside the spacecraft may wear a maneuvering unit called a **jet-pack**. Jets of nitrogen from a compressed-nitrogen tank are squirted from sets of nozzles, using hand controls. In this way the astronaut can move in all three dimensions: up/down, left/right, and forward/backward. But there is no air to slow the astronaut, so he or she must squirt a jet of nitrogen in the opposite direction in order to stop moving.

Satellites can be launched from the spacecraft's cargo bay using a remote-controlled **robot arm** to position them precisely in orbit. Satellites which are broken or out of position can be captured by the arm.

Nitrogen tank

Nitrogen supply

Thrusters directed in three dimensions

Satellite's grip post

Orbiter's arm clamp

Remote-control arm

Flight deck

Cargo bay

Cargo doors open

SPACE SHUTTLE

Rockets such as *Ariane* and *Apollo V*, which launched the manned mooncrafts in the 1960s and 70s, are ELV's or Expendable Launch Vehicles. They are designed for use only once, and their parts fall to Earth or burn up in the atmosphere. The Space Shuttle is an RLV – a reusable launch vehicle. The part that goes into space, the ''spaceplane'' itself, is known as the orbiter. At lift-off, it is helped by two solid-fuel boosters, each 150 feet long and producing 1,200 tons of thrust. These fall away after 2 minutes and 12 seconds. Fuel for the orbiter's three main engines is contained in a gigantic

fuel tank 154 feet long, which is emptied and falls away 8 minutes and 50 seconds after lift-off. At launch, the weight of the orbiter, boosters and fuel tank is 2,000 tons! The orbiter has a wingspan of 78 feet and is 122 feet long. It travels around Earth at heights of 60 to 185 miles. Two pilots fly the orbiter from the flight deck. Other crew members are the mission specialists, who carry out experiments in space or help to launch and capture satellites.

Fin

Orbiter's fuel tank

Rudder/air brake

Orbiter's three rocket engines

Wing

In order to move about in space, the astronaut wears a personal spacecraft – the **spacesuit**. This has an inner water-cooled suit and an outer pressure-suit that protects against the sun's glare and radiation and also against the tiny meteorites (fragments of rock or metal) that speed through space. The backpack provides oxygen to breathe and circulates cooling water around the inner suit.

Airtight seals

Helmet and visor

Inner suit

Outer suit

After launch, the orbiter usually stays in space for several days. At the end of the mission, it comes back down into Earth's atmosphere at tremendous speed, and friction with the ever-thickening air creates enormous heat. The orbiter is protected from burning up by special ceramic tiles fixed to the lower fuselage. As it comes in to land on the runway, the Shuttle is the world's biggest glider.

Boosters released

Fuel tank released

RE-ENTRY

Parachute

Glide-down

LIFT-OFF

LANDING

THE BUILDING SITE

TOWER CRANE 3

DRILLING AND PILEDRIVING 4

ELEVATOR 8

RIVETS AND WELDS 5

DIGGER 2

CONCRETE MIXER 6

SPIRIT LEVEL 7

UNDERGROUND SERVICES 1

2 DIGGER

The multipurpose digger makes trenches and holes, loads materials into trucks, and can bulldoze areas level. The arms, and their buckets, are operated by hydraulic pistons. As hydraulic fluid is pumped under great pressure into the cylinder, it pushes the piston along. The piston is connected to a lever that moves the arm or bucket. These hydraulic pistons can only push. Like the muscles in the human body they are arranged in opposing pairs.

Piston

High-pressure seal

Slave cylinder

Hydraulic fluid

Stabilizing stands

3 TOWER CRANE

Towering over the building site, this crane can lift objects over a large area. Its main arm, or jib, swivels around, and the hook-carrying trolley is pulled, or winched, along the jib by cables and a motor. The crane is self-erecting. After its base is installed, it uses a special extending section, into which it fits a new section of tower. The extending section then "crawls" up the tower section, fits another tower section into itself and so on, until it is the correct height.

Operator's cab

Hoist

Main jib

Trolley winch

Counter-weight

Hook and pulley system

FINAL HEIGHT REACHED

TOWER SECTION FITTED

EXTENDING SECTION FITTED

UNDERGROUND SERVICES

Under the city streets is a maze of tunnels, pipes, wires and cables, known collectively as services. They include underground gas pipes, telephone lines and water mains. Before any new building is erected, planners must check with the city records office to see where they can and cannot dig. They must also look for places where they can tap into services for the new building.

Sewers

Water main

Electricity

Telecommunications

Gas

4. DRILLING AND PILEDRIVING

To keep a building from toppling, cracking or sinking, it must be built on firm foundations. The taller the building, the deeper the foundations. Columns or piles can be sunk deep into the ground by drilling or driving. The piledriver is a large weight that is repeatedly raised and dropped onto a driving wedge or pile, hammering it deep into the earth. The earth auger, a rotary device in a derrick tower, works like an oil rig drill (page 63). The World Trade Center in New York City has foundations 70 feet deep.

Pile tower

Piling weight raised and dropped
Pile rammed into ground

PILEDRIVING

DRILLING

Drilling derrick

Drill shaft

H-section girder fitted into hole

Drill bit rotates

Girder concreted in

5. RIVETS AND WELDS

There are numerous ways of joining girders, plates and other pieces of buildings and machinery. These include screws, nuts and bolts, adhesives, rivets and welds. A rivet is a metal pin with a flattened head at one end. It is pushed by its flat head into holes in the parts to be fastened. A rivet gun then hammers the other

Holes prepared in two plates

Rivet gun flattens end of rivet

Steel rivet

Plates secured together

6. CONCRETE MIXER

In a premixed concrete truck, the Archimedes screw keeps the concrete or mortar circulating as it is carried from the mixing depot to the building site. The screw is essentially a spiral or helical ramp (page 25) wound around inside a drum. The same device was used in ancient Egypt to lift water out of ditches for irrigating the fields beyond.

Concrete kept moving and mixing

Archimedes screw inside drum

Drive shaft from engine

end flat, squeezing and securing the parts together.

In a weld, the very high temperature created by an electric arc or flame melts the two metal parts at the join. The liquefied metals run together, and after the heat is removed they solidify and fuse together.

Steam given off

Oxygen feed

Hydrogen feed

Welding head

Metal plates melt together

Intense heat at welding flame

7 SPIRIT LEVEL

In the spirit level, a bubble of air floats in oil or a spirit-based fluid inside a transparent container. The air, being much less dense than the fluid, always finds the highest part of the container and floats on top of the fluid. When the device is level, the bubble rests in the middle of the container, midway between the two marks.

Air bubble

Level marks

Oil chamber

Flat-sided casing

Not level

Level

8 ELEVATOR

The goods and materials elevator on a building site works in the same way as the passenger elevator inside a tall building. The elevator car runs up and down a guide tower, or between the guide rails of an elevator shaft. It is winched up by the lifting motor, which does not have to lift the whole weight of the car since this is balanced by a counterweight. A safety brake locks the car to the rails or tower if the cable snaps.

Control and switching gear

Lifting motor

Winch drum

Main cable

Elevator car

Guide rail

Safety brake

Counterweight rises as elevator descends

Floor buffer

BRIDGES

SPANNING THE RIVER
2

TYPES OF BRIDGES
1

NUTS AND BOLTS
3

1

TYPES OF BRIDGES

Four main types of bridge design are shown on the right. Each has advantages. The beam design can be simple and inexpensive, but it needs regular supports along its length. It is not suitable for a wide, deep river. In the cantilever design, each pair of side spans projects beyond their supporting tower, balancing each other for better stability.

Beam

Single-span arch

Suspension

Cantilever

2 SPANNING THE RIVER

In a suspension bridge, the deck hangs by suspending cables from the enormously thick main cables. New York's Verrazano-Narrows Bridge has four main cables, each three feet thick, spun from hundreds of thinner steel wires. The main cables transmit the pull of the roadway over the towers to the cable anchorages in the ground at either end.

The world's longest single-span suspension bridge is 4626 feet long, over the Humber Estuary in northeastern England.

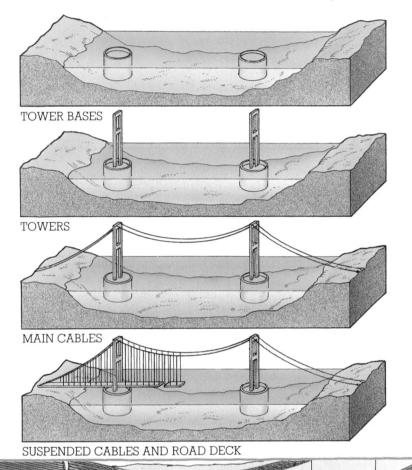

TOWER BASES

TOWERS

MAIN CABLES

SUSPENDED CABLES AND ROAD DECK

3 NUTS AND BOLTS

The thread of a bolt winds around the shaft in a helical pattern. (A screw thread has a spiral pattern, page 25.) As it turns, it works like a ramp to force the nut along its length. This changes a rotary force into a longitudinal (lengthwise) force.

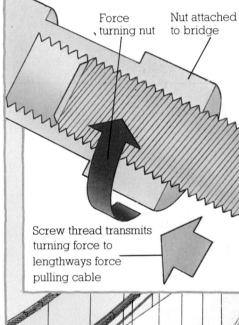

Force turning nut

Nut attached to bridge

Screw thread transmits turning force to lengthways force pulling cable

4

Marker rule

Angle measured between marks on rule

Theodolite

THEODOLITE

This surveying instrument measures angles. It is mounted on an adjustable tripod, and it has spirit levels (page 55) to show when it is horizontal. The main target is sighted through the eyepiece of the main telescope. A second eyepiece is aimed at the second target, and the angle between these two lines of sight is read off. The surveyor then uses the geometry of triangles to calculate distances and other measurements.

TUNNELS

PISTON RELIEF DUCT
3

FIRE DETECTOR
6

DO-DO TRAIN
5

FIRE EXTINGUISHER
7

TUNNEL STRUCTURE
1

SUMP PUMP
4

1 TUNNEL STRUCTURE

The Eurotunnel between England and France is, in fact, three tunnels. The two main shafts, each 25 feet across, will convey locomotives carrying vehicles and passengers. Between them is the smaller service tunnel, 16 feet in diameter. This will carry services such as electrical cables and water pipes. It will also be used for access and maintenance, and escape in emergencies.

Piston relief duct

Central safety and access tunnel

Twin main tunnels

Dover, England

Route of channel tunnel

Calais, France

Clay layer   The Channel   Chalk layer

Sea

2 TUNNEL-BORING MACHINE

TUNNEL-BORING MACHINE

TUNNEL-BORING MACHINE

Eurotunnel's rotating cutter head is like a giant drill (page 27). It bears over 100 cutting rollers to chew up the rock, and 200 teeth, made of the very hard metal tungsten. The head goes around about twice each minute, depending on the material being drilled. Hydraulic rams guide the cutting head, steered by laser beams. The gripper ring pushes against the tunnel wall as rams force the machine forward. A system of conveyors takes away the spoil at a rate of 2,472 cubic feet (almost two large dump trucks) for every 3 feet of tunnel drilled.

3 PISTON RELIEF DUCT

As a train travels through the Eurotunnel at 100 miles per hour, it will push air in front of it. This will gradually increase the air pressure, like air being forced along a cylinder by a piston (page 89). It could even damage passengers' ears. So there are regular smaller cross-shafts, known as *piston relief ducts*, between the two main tunnels. Air pushed by the speeding locomotive will circulate through the ducts, back along the other tunnel, and then into the main tunnel behind the locomotive. In this way the pressure build-up is avoided.

Piston relief duct

Air flows back along other tunnel

Piston relief duct

High-pressure wave in front of train

Air flows back into tunnel and equalizes pressure

4 SUMP PUMP

It is impossible to prevent rainwater, drips of oil and fuel, and various other fluids from collecting along the tunnel bottoms. Among other problems, this could create a fire hazard. The sump pump is specially designed to collect these various wastes. It is worked by high-pressure water that rotates the vanes and draws up the wastes, to be pumped away along the outlet pipe.

Wastes and water pumped out

Outlet pipe

Water inlet

Impeller

Diffuser

5 DO-DO TRAIN

With the fastest trip under the English Channel taking only 35 minutes, loading and unloading could take up a large proportion of the total journey time. So, like the ro-ro ferry (page 42), the do-do train is designed for a speedy and convenient turnaround of vehicles and freight. Cars can "Drive On and Drive Off" without having to be loaded by cranes or turned around

6 FIRE DETECTOR

The fire detectors are fitted at regular intervals along the tunnel. They contain a specially developed *alloy* (mixture of metals) that melts at temperatures only a little above normal. The melted blob completes an electric circuit and sets off the alarm.

Power source

Alarm

Circuit wiring

Electric wire

Alloy in thimble

Melted alloy completes circuit to set off alarm

Heat sensor

HEAT

7 FIRE EXTINGUISHER

The carbon dioxide (CO_2) type of extinguisher is most common. When the strike knob is hit, the piercer punctures the pressure-release disk and allows the pressurized carbon dioxide to escape. This gas is heavier than air and it settles over the fire, smothering it like a blanket and keeping away the oxygen that flames need in order to burn. Deprived of oxygen, the fire gradually goes out.

Carbon dioxide "blanket" smothers fire

Directing tube

Strike knob

Piercer

Pressure release disk

Carbon dioxide

Pressurized powder and carbon dioxide

Central tube

ın the cars. Eurotunnel's passenger cars are 82 feet long. There are about 30 in the standard tourist shuttle train that travels back and forth between the two terminals.

The freight cars are 59 feet long and each train consists of about 25 of them. There will also be bulk-freight cars to carry loads such as grain.

1. High-speed electric locomotive

2. Trucks and container-freight loading bay

3. Upper car deck loading ramp

4. Lower car deck loading ramp

5. High and special loads

OIL EXPLORATION

DRILLING RI[G] 2

RIGS AND PLATFORMS 1

EXPLORATION RIG 3

HELICOPTER 6

DIVING EQUIPMENT 4

PRODUCTION PLATFORM 5

1 RIGS AND PLATFORMS

Some of the biggest structures ever made are oil rigs and platforms. An oilfield under the ground can be tapped by many small wells, which are constructed on site. For oilfields under the sea, specialized platforms are required. In deep water, the platforms float and are kept in place by anchoring chains. In shallow water they can lower their legs to stand on the seabed. Various ways of doing this are illustrated (*right*). The largest oil platform is the Statfjord B platform in the North Sea. At 885 feet, it is taller than a 70-story building.

Legs jacked up   Rig reaches station   Legs lowered

Rig floated on side
Towed to station   Legs flood and
rig tips upright

Towed to station   Tanks flood and sink

2 DRILLING RIG

The drilling derrick is a tower that supports the drill pipes. As the drill bit is gradually lowered, extra lengths of pipe are attached to the top pipe, called the kelly. The kelly also raises the drill pipes section by section when the drill bit needs to be changed. The drill pipes contain several channels (*right*). A special mixture of mud is pumped at high pressure down one channel. It cools and lubricates the rotary drill bit (*far right*) and carries pieces of drilled rock back up to the surface through the outer pipe channel. The high-pressure mud also prevents underground water from leaking into the borehole. Once the oil-bearing rocks are reached (*below left*), the drilling pipes are withdrawn and casing pipes are inserted into the bore. These form the tube up which the oil flows to the surface. Sometimes powerful acids or explosives are used to start the oil flowing.

Diamond drill bit for grinding rocks

Roller drill bit for crushing rocks

Outer casing

Inner casing

Drill rotates

Drill derrick

Monkey board

Kelly

Oil-bearing rocks

Monkey board

Kelly lowered

Mud pump

Rotary table

Kelly raised

New length of drill pipe added

Inner channel

Outer channel

Mud pumped down

Spoil-containing slurry forced up

Drill bit

3 EXPLORATION RIG

Searching for oil (petroleum) is immensely costly. Before drilling starts, scientists study the seabed and the underground rocks, using techniques of *seismology* and other earth sciences to see if they are likely to contain oil. Then the smaller, mobile exploration rig drills a series of test bores, to mark out the extent and depth of the oilfield. If there is enough oil to make extraction worthwhile, a production platform is installed (*opposite*).

Present drill site

Exploratory rig

Past drill sites

Extent of oil field

Rock strata

4 DIVING EQUIPMENT

The underwater parts of oil rigs, drills and pipelines must be checked for corrosion, maintained and serviced. Highly trained divers carry out this hazardous work. They can descend to depths of more than 300 feet with special scuba gear. (Scuba stands for Self-Contained Underwater Breathing Apparatus.) The scuba's breathing mechanism is shown on the right. As the diver breathes in, gas from the aqualung's pressure tank passes through valves and a diaphragm which form an airlock to reduce its pressure. Breathed-out gases bubble into the water.

BREATHING IN

Diaphragm bends down

First stage valve closed

Second stage valve open

BREATHING OUT

Air tube

Mouthpiece

Air into mouth

Diaphragm bends up

PRODUCTION PLATFORM

Oil under great pressure wells up the borehole to the production platform. Its pressure and flow rate are controlled by a complex system of valves and pipes known as the Christmas tree. For an oilfield on land or near the coast, the oil can be fed into a pipeline to the refinery (page 106). Offshore, huge tankers collect the oil from storage vessels (*below*) and take it to the refinery. Several boreholes help to equalize pressure across the oilfield (*below right*).

Whipstock

Well

Tanker being loaded

Storage buoy

Production platform

Angled drill formation

Seabed pipeline

Storage tanks

Water pressure increases by one atmosphere (the average air pressure at sea level) for every 33 feet of depth. Below about 330 feet (130 feet for an ordinary scuba setup), the water pressure on the human body is too great for safe scuba diving. The all-enclosing deep-sea pressure suit must then be used. Like a spacesuit (page 51), it has joints in the limbs and has porthole windows through which the diver looks. Air, or a special mixture of gases for deep diving, is contained in its tanks. The diver can communicate with surface workers by microphone and headphones. Suits such as these can descend to 1968 feet.

Security tether and microphone cable

Pressurized helmet

Windows

Hand claw

Pressurized suit

Joints in arms and legs

6 HELICOPTER

Helicopters are used to ferry supplies and people to oil rigs, and also to rescue them in an emergency (as shown here). They can fly backward, forward, both up and down and also remain hovering stationary in the air. Instead of a fixed wing, helicopters have a set of rotating blades which act as long, thin wings. These rotor blades can be tilted to control the helicopter's direction. The pilot's control stick alters the angle of the blades via a rotating swash plate. The diagram below shows how the pilot's controls are connected to the swash plate and then to the rotor blades.

The rotors spin around very fast in one direction and the natural reaction is for the rest of the machine to spin around in the opposite direction. A small rotor mounted on the tail acts as a propeller whose thrust cancels out this tendency. Some helicopters have two sets of main rotors that spin in opposite directions, so each blade cancels the spinning force of the other.

Unlike airplanes, helicopters have no natural stability. They require constant adjustments to the controls to keep them in level flight.

Blade rotation

Rotor blade

Pitch arm

Connecting rod

Rotating swash plate

Lower swash plate (does not rotate)

Direction control rods

Turboshaft engine

Bearings

THE ROTOR HEAD

Rotor shaft

THE CONTROLS

Cyclic control stick

Collective pitch control lever

Directional control pedals

THE TAIL ROTOR

Tail rotor direction

Tail plane

Tail rotor transmission shaft

MANEUVERING

To take off and hover the helicopter pilot pulls the collective pitch control lever. This increases the lift of the main rotor blades. The lift is directed downward and the helicopter rises straight up. To fly ahead the pilot pushes the cyclic control stick forward. This increases the lift of the blades as they pass behind the pilot and decreases their lift when they come forward. The helicopter tilts its nose down and the rearward thrust pushes it along.

UP

FORWARD

RIGHT

Direction

Rotor force

Tail rotor force

Engine force

CREATING LIFT

The shape of the helicopter's rotor forces air to pass over the top surface faster than it does below. The air pressure above the rotor falls and the helicopter is pushed upward. Since the pressure rises equally below the rotor blades, the helicopter can also be thought of as riding on a bed of compressed air. To fly higher the pilot tilts the blades, making air flow even faster across the top surface. This increases the lifting force and pushes the helicopter higher.

Lift

Rotor direction

Air flow faster

Air flow slower

Rotor blade

POWER STATIONS

NUCLEAR POWER STATION 3

ELECTRICITY DISTRIBUTION 2

TIDAL POWER STATION 7

STEAM TURBINES 4

COAL-FIRED POWER STATION 1

GENERATOR 5

HYDROELECTRIC POWER 6

1 COAL-FIRED POWER STATION

A power station converts one form of energy, such as the chemical bonds in coal or the energy of moving water, into electricity. In the coal-fired power station, coal is burned at a great temperature in a furnace, liberating heat. The heat turns water in the boiler into high-pressure steam. This rushes through turbines and makes them spin (page 71), and the spinning motion turns a generator which makes the electricity. The hot water is cooled for recycling in the large cooling towers.

Stack

Precipitator, removes dirt and grit from the smoke

Coal hopper

Coal conveyor

Pulverizing mill

ELECTRICITY DISTRIBUTION

Large amounts of electricity are carried by overhead lines at very high voltages – 500 million volts or more. (High voltages lose less power when carried over long distances.) Substation transformers change the voltage to a few thousand volts, and then to about 110 or 220–240 volts for home use. The transformer works by *inductance*. If the output coil has twice as many windings as the input coil, it produces twice the voltage – but at only half the current. The total power, measured in *watts* (which equals volts multiplied by amps), stays the same.

Three windings   Metal core   Six windings

TRANSFORMER

100 volts at 10 amps

200 volts at 5 amps

Transformers and switching gear

High-voltage lines on pylons   Substation

Medium-voltage underground cables

Low-voltage domestic supply

Power station

Transformer

Boiler

Burners

Air intake

Turbine

Condenser

Generator

Cooling tower

Warm air

Cool air

Cool water

Hot water

NUCLEAR POWER STATION

3

The various designs of nuclear power stations work on the principle that tiny amounts of matter can be changed into enormous quantities of energy. A nucleus is the small, dense, central part of each atom. The nuclei of certain substances are unstable and ready to split (called nuclear fission) if stimulated in some way. The stimulus can be bombardment by other atomic particles or rays. When this happens, the nucleus splits into two or more parts. The total mass, or weight, of these parts does not add up to the mass of the original intact nucleus. The difference in mass appears as heat energy. For example, if the nucleus of uranium-235 is hit by one neutron particle, it splits into two other substances (krypton and barium), plus energy, plus about two more neutrons. These neutrons continue the reaction by splitting more uranium-235 nuclei, and so on, in a chain reaction. The reaction is stopped from getting out of hand by control rods that absorb extra neutrons.

Atomic nucleus

Atomic nucleus splits

HEAT AND RADIATION

Reaction continues as more nuclei split

Hot water

Primary circuit

Heat exchanger

Steam to turbines

Fuel rod

Control rod

Reactor core

Pressure vessel and radiation shielding

Cooled water

Secondary circuit

Core casing

Nuclei split

Some nuclei absorbed

REACTOR CORE

STEAM TURBINES

Turbines are fan-like blades mounted on a central shaft. Because they are set at an angle, they turn when a fluid (liquid or gas) flows past them. The principle is the same as when you blow at a toy windmill. Your breath is like the steam, and the windmill sails act like turbine blades. Steam turbines are spun by high-pressure steam produced from boiling water, which has been heated in the boiler of a power station. As the steam loses pressure, it flows past different sizes and angles of blades, each designed to extract the maximum energy from the steam at that point. The central shaft of the turbines is connected to the generator (*below*).

High-pressure steam in

First turbine

Second turbine

Third turbine

Mid-pressure steam

Low-pressure steam

Drive shafts

Steam out to condensers

GENERATOR

The mechanical energy of a spinning shaft is converted into electrical energy by this device. A central magnet, or rotor, turns around inside a series of electrical coils, called the *stator*. As the magnetic field of the rotor passes through the stator coils, it creates electricity in the windings, by inductance. The rotor is an electromagnet that itself needs electricity to make its magnetic field. This is conveyed to its own coils by brushes that press against slip-rings on the spinning shaft. But it is a small amount of electricity compared to the total quantity generated.

Casing

Magnets on rotor

Windings on stator

Brushes

Drive shaft

ELECTRICITY GENERATED

6

HYDROELECTRIC POWER STATION

The force of gravity pulls water along a river to the sea. The hydroelectric power station taps into this flow of falling water and uses it to turn turbine blades. Under the turbine is a *draft tube* that allows water to fall away from the blades quickly. This creates a vacuum effect that sucks more water in, thereby increasing the efficiency of the turbine. The turbine is connected to electricity generators. A river that is in full flood in the wet season but then shrinks in the dry season is too unreliable by itself for hydroelectricity. Therefore a dam is usually built at the site. This holds back the water in times of plenty and uses this stored water to drive the turbines during dry spells. The dam creates a lake behind it which makes water available for irrigation. Three-quarters of South America's electricity is hydroelectricity. This type of power generation does not pollute the atmosphere like a coal-fired station, and it does not create hazardous and long-lasting radioactive wastes as do nuclear power stations.

Roadway

Screens and filters

Sluice gates

Concrete shell

Riprap
(broken stones)

Concrete tunnel under dam

Turbines

One design of hydroelectric turbine is the Francis reaction turbine (*below*). Water pushes the blades around as it streams through the adjustable vanes and then falls downward. Another design, the Kaplan turbine, looks like a ship's propeller (page 40).

Windings on stator

Magnets on rotor

Electrical cables

Connecting shaft

WATER IN

Turbine blades

WATER OUT

Power house

High-voltage power lines

Water outlet

7

TIDAL POWER STATION

The sun and the moon both pull on the earth due to their gravitational forces. The movements of the earth around the sun, and the moon around the earth, pull bulges of seawater around our planet. As a bulge passes a certain place on the shore, we call it a high tide. The trough before the next bulge is the low tide. Tides can be turned into electricity by a tidal power station that operates in a similar way to the hydroelectric power station (*opposite*). The dam for the turbines is built at the coast, across the mouth of a river. As the tide rises, seawater flows through the dam tunnels into the river and spins the turbines. When the tide flows out, the turbine blades spin in the other direction.

Roadway on barrage   Sluice gates open

Rising tide

Water flows through turbines

Falling tide

Water trapped behind barrage

73

THE NEWSROOM

BINOCULARS 7

OPTICAL FIBER 2

COMPUTER PRINTERS 6

TELEPHONE 1

BALLPOINT PEN 4

FAX MACH

MOBILE PHONE 3

SLR CAMERA 8

1

TELEPHONE

The microphone and loudspeakers in a stereo system (page 135) deal with a wide range of tones, from bass drum to piccolo. But the telephone handles a relatively small range of tones, centered on the pitch of the human voice. Its working parts are therefore small and of simple construction. In the mouthpiece, sound waves vibrate the diaphragm, which compresses a packet of carbon granules. This alters the flow of electricity through the granules, producing signals that travel to the listener's earpiece.

Signals travel both ways to each phone

Telephone exchange

MOUTHPIECE

EARPIECE
Diaphragm
Armature
Wiring coils

Electromagnet
Diaphragm
Carbon granules
Electrical current

2 OPTICAL FIBER

Inside an optical fiber, light rays reflect repeatedly off the inner surface. They can travel around bends as a series of short straight lines. Many telephone networks now use optical fibers. These hair-thin fibers can carry more light signals more efficiently than electrical signals in a wire.

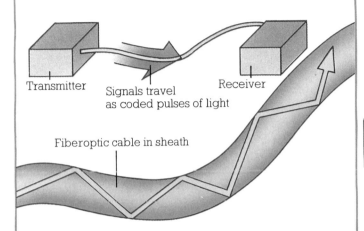

Transmitter

Signals travel as coded pulses of light

Receiver

Fiberoptic cable in sheath

3 MOBILE PHONE

An area covered by a cellular phone network is divided into a number of smaller areas, or cells. Each cell has a transceiver (transmitter/receiver) station. The mobile phone sends and receives messages by radio waves. The signals travel between stations via the standard telephone network.

Transceiver dish

Signals to/from aerial

Nearest station

Nearest station

4 BALLPOINT PEN

Oil-based ink flows down the refill tube onto the ball as it rotates, and it spreads onto the paper beneath. The ball and its seating are made from very hard metals, such as tungsten, to minimize wear.

Ball bearing tip

Ink

Case

Refill tube

Alloy seating

5 FAX MACHINE

Fax is short for facsimile, which means a copy or reproduction. The fax machine both sends and receives. It can transmit any marks on paper, from a sketchy drawing to typeset words (page 78). The scanner "reads" the paper line by line, detecting any dark patches and coding these as electrical signals. The signals travel via the telephone network to the receiving machine. There, a printer puts the same pattern of marks as tiny dots onto the paper – a fraction of a second later.

SENDING

Decoding unit

Coding unit

RECEIVING

Scanner tracks along each line

Heat-sensitive paper

Drive motor

Rotating drum scrolls paper

Print head tracks along each line

6 COMPUTER PRINTERS

In the printout from a dot-matrix printer, the words or pictures are made up of patterns of tiny dots. These dots are made by little pins in the print head, which hammer against an inked ribbon as the head whizzes along, line by line, making ink spots on the paper. The pins are worked by miniature electromagnets. In a daisy-wheel printer, each letter or number is a raised ridge on the print head. The wheel twirls around until the correct letter is aligned with the hammer, which then punches it against an inked ribbon to mark the paper. The wheel spokes are supposed to resemble the petals of a daisy, hence the name.

DOT-MATRIX PRINTER

Pins

Print head tracks along each line

Print head

Flexible spoke

Daisy wheel

Hub with aligning cog

DAISY-WHEEL PRINTER

Hammer worked by electromagnet

Wheel spins for different letters

7 BINOCULARS

A telescope gives a two-dimensional image with no depth, but a pair of binoculars lets you see in three dimensions. Each barrel contains a lens system that magnifies the view and prisms that bend the light rays, thereby allowing the barrel to be quite short. The prisms also turn the image the correct way up for the eye. Look through one eyepiece only, and you see a flat scene as if through a telescope. When you look through both barrels, your brain combines the slightly different view from each eye into one three-dimensional scene, just as it does in normal sight.

Eyepiece lens system

Prism

Prism

Barrel

Objective lens system

LIGHT

8

SLR CAMERA

SLR means Single Lens Reflex. The "single lens" refers to the fact that the scene through the viewfinder is exactly the same as the scene that appears on the film, because they are both seen through the same lens. (In some cameras, the viewfinder has a separate lens, to one side of the main lens.) A mirror in front of the film reflects light rays up to a five-sided pentaprism. The prism turns the image the correct way up by reflecting the light rays around a series of corners – this is the "reflex" part. It then sends the rays on to the eye. When the shutter button is pressed, the mirror swings up out of the way. The light rays momentarily fall onto the film before the mirror swings down again.

Shutter button
Focusing plate
Prism
Spool winder
Eyepiece
Film
Aperture ring
Focusing ring
Mirror
Diaphragm aperture control
LIGHT
Objective lens system

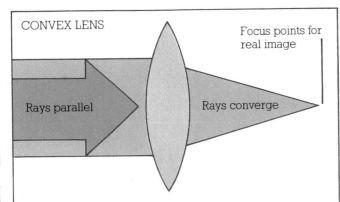

CONVEX LENS

Focus points for real image

Rays parallel

Rays converge

The two basic lens types are concave lenses and convex lenses. As light rays pass from the air into the glass of the lens, they are bent slightly or *refracted*. They are refracted again as they leave the glass and enter the air on the other side of the lens. The curvature of a convex lens bends the rays inward, making them converge.

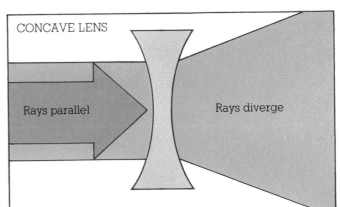

CONCAVE LENS

Rays parallel

Rays diverge

The curved surfaces of the concave lens diverge the light rays, bending them outward. Lenses are vital to optical instruments such as cameras, binoculars, telescopes and microscopes. Such lenses are usually made from special optical glass. They are arranged in groups, called lens systems, to reduce image distortion.

PRINTING A BOOK

TYPESETTER 1

COLOR SCANNER 2

PRINTING METHODS 3

COLOR PRINTING 4

PRINTING PRESS 5

PHOTOCOPIER 6

1 TYPESETTER

Printed words like the ones you are reading now are the result of a series of processes, starting with the typesetter. This machine stores in its computer memory the sizes and shapes of various typefaces – the different styles and designs of letters and numbers. The words in this book are in the typeface called Rockwell.

To typeset the letters, the computer controls the movements of a laser beam that etches the shapes of the letters onto a rotating drum of special printing paper or printing film (page 80). Highly magnified, the letters are seen to be made up of numerous lines (*below right*).

Computer

Laser beam

Photographic paper

Letter made from lines

Laser "draws" lines on bromide paper or film

Keyboard input

Revolving drum

2 COLOR SCANNER

To prepare a color photograph or illustration for printing, it must first be separated into its primary colors so that each may be printed separately (page 80). This is a job for the color scanner. The laser beam scans line by line as the photograph revolves on a drum. During each scan the frequency of the light in the laser is changed to correspond with each of the primary colors, so that it detects only the parts of the photograph which are of that particular color. This is repeated four times: once for each of the three primary colors (cyan [blue], magenta [red] and yellow), and once for black. The information about which colors are where on the photograph is coded as electrical signals. It can be converted into four separate printing films or stored in a computer memory.

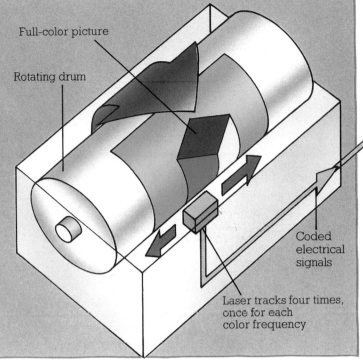

Full-color picture

Rotating drum

Coded electrical signals

Laser tracks four times, once for each color frequency

3 PRINTING METHODS

Since the German goldsmith Johann Gutenberg invented the first proper printing press, in about 1450, there have been various developments in printing techniques. Four methods of printing are shown here. Each depends on passing paper over an inked roller or plate, so that the ink comes off the roller or plate and sticks to the paper. The offset lithography press is described on page 80. In letterpress, the image exists as a raised area on a lower base. Only the raised part receives the printing ink. In gravure, the image is a shallow "hole" below the surface of the plate or roller, and ink is scraped from the raised, non-printing part by a doctor blade. Silkscreen printing involves forcing ink through a very fine net-like screen onto the paper; the shape of the stencil forms the image.

OFFSET LITHO

Grease-based ink rollers
Greasy image
Paper
Printed image
Damping rollers
Rubber blanket
Pressure roller

LETTERPRESS

Pressure roller
Paper
Printed image
Raised image inked
Ink rollers

GRAVURE

Printed image
Paper
Print area (below surface)
Doctor blade
Ink bath

SILKSCREEN

Frame
Screen and mask
Squeegee sponge spreads ink
Ink
Printed image

4 COLOR PRINTING

The color pictures in this book are made from patterns of tiny ink dots. There are four colors of dots. These are the three primary printing colors of cyan, magenta and yellow, plus black. Each is printed from a separate piece of printing film on the press (*shown below*). From a distance, the eye sees the separate dots as areas of continuous ink. It also merges the different combinations of primary colors to see all the other colors of the spectrum.

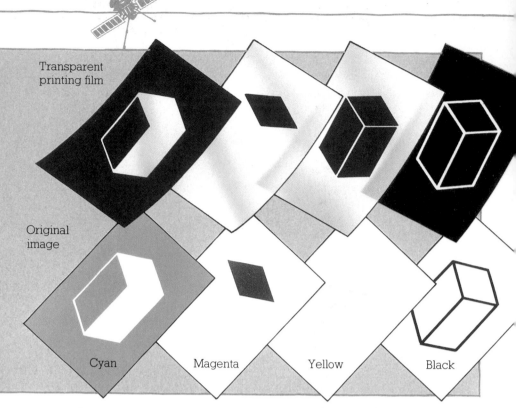

Transparent printing film

Original image

Cyan   Magenta   Yellow   Black

5 PRINTING PRESS

On the offset lithography press, each primary color is printed separately. The image on the plate or roller exists as a part of its surface that has been treated, or "etched," to attract grease-based printing ink and to repel water. For areas that are not to be printed, the surface is treated to attract water but to repel the greasy ink. The ink roller puts ink onto the image parts of the surface, while the damping rollers put water onto the nonprinting areas. The ink is then transferred to another, intermediate roller bearing a rubber blanket. This presses the ink onto the paper. "Offset" refers to the transfer of the inked image to an intermediate roller.

Reel of paper

Web

Ink feed

Yellow unit

Black unit

Oscillating rollers

Tension controls

Coolant circuit

OFFSET PRESS

Cyan unit

Magenta unit

To cutting, collating, binding

Extra unit for special colors (metallic gold, silver) or varnishes

6 PHOTOCOPIER

This fairly recent method of copy-printing is suitable for a few tens or perhaps hundreds of copies. But it becomes expensive for larger numbers, compared with other printing processes. Photocopying is based on the principle that static electricity attracts objects. This happens when you rub a balloon on a dry woolen sweater. The friction of rubbing generates static electricity that makes the balloon stick to the sweater. The photocopier has a large electrostatic drum that is charged with static electricity in the same way. The image to be copied is beamed down from the platen onto the drum by a series of mirrors and lenses, and it alters the pattern of charges. The charged parts attract the toner, usually granules of ink. This is transferred to a sheet of paper and then fixed in place, usually by heat.

Image to be copied

Moving platen   Mirror   Lamp   Lens   Mirrors

Copied image

Toner brush

First erase lamp

Paper-feed roller

Plain paper supply

Electrostatic drum   Heater   Feed-out rollers

Second erase lamp   Carrier belt

THE TELEVISION STUDIO

SATELLITE TELEVISION 5

RHEOSTAT 3

ANIMATION 4

TELEVISION CAMERA 2

TELEPROMPTER 1

---

1 **TELEPROMPTER**

Imagine being in a brightly lit room when it is almost dark outside. Look at the window. You can see both the scene outside, through the glass, and the things inside the room, reflected in the glass. The teleprompter machine works along the same lines. There is a glass sheet between the newscaster and the screen. The camera "sees" the newscaster through the glass. The newscaster sees the camera – and also the reflections of the words on the monitor screen. Are the words on the screen upside down, or in mirror writing?

Special transmission-reflecting glass

TV camera

Newscaster

Light from screen reflects off glass to eyes

Light from face to camera passes through glass

Text scrolls on screen

Teleprompter monitor

TELEVISION CAMERA

White light is made up of a mixture of different colors that can be separated by a prism to form the colors of the spectrum. The prism in one type of television camera is designed to split light from the scene into three colors: red, green and blue. It does this by *refraction*. Each color of light consists of rays of a slightly different wavelength. The different wavelengths are refracted by slightly different amounts as they pass into and out of the glass of the prism.

The angles of the prism's faces are arranged so that the three main colors are separated from each other and shine out of the prism in different directions. Each color is beamed into a detector that scans the image and converts the patterns of light rays into electrical signals. The camera operator watches the scene through the viewfinder, a small TV screen mounted on the camera. In the television set, the three colors are recombined on the screen (page 131).

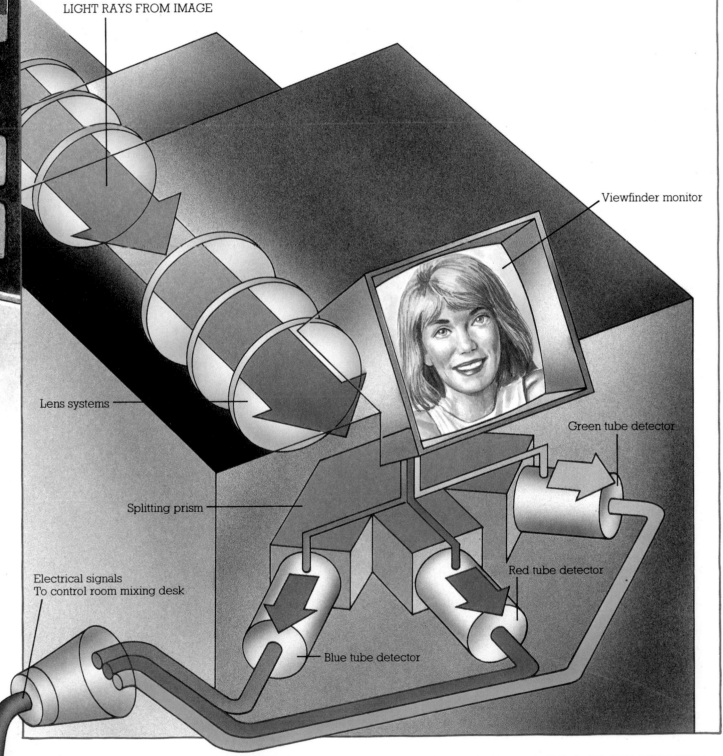

LIGHT RAYS FROM IMAGE

Viewfinder monitor

Lens systems

Green tube detector

Splitting prism

Red tube detector

Electrical signals
To control room mixing desk

Blue tube detector

3 RHEOSTAT

Many of the knobs and switches on electrical equipment operate adjustable resistors, or dimmers, called rheostats. The basic rheostat is a coil of resistance wire touched by a sliding contact on one side, which forms part of an electrical circuit. When the electricity passes through only a few turns of the coil, it meets only a slight resistance. If the contact is slid to the other end, there is much more resistance wire included in the circuit, and the electricity is thereby reduced. A similar device works by turning a metal wiper around an arc-shaped resistance bar to tap off varying amounts of electricity.

B: LESS RESISTANCE

Dimmer switch

Electrical power source

Wire

Rheostat coil of resistance wire

Sliding contact touches strip of bared wire on windings

A: MORE RESISTANCE

A: LAMP DIMS
B: LAMP BRIGHTENS

4 ANIMATION

A television or movie screen does not show a continuously moving image. It shows a number of still images in rapid succession, many each second. The eye blurs together these quickly changing still images and sees them as a "moving picture." Animation is the technique of making a moving picture from a series of still images created by artists, or by models, or photographs, or computerized graphics. Cartoons are one familiar example. Each image, or frame, is drawn and colored as a separate piece of artwork. The images are recorded one by one, as individual frames on film or videotape (pages 132, 139). When played back at normal speed, the frames blur together and create the illusion of movement.

One-shot camera

Light

Adjustable cradle

Cover

Platen

Raise/lower wheel

Camera support

Single frame from sequence

5 SATELLITE TELEVISION

A broadcasting aerial on the ground can beam signals only a limited distance. Even if the aerial is on a tall mast, hills and valleys in the landscape can soon block the signals. The TV satellite can be thought of as an aerial on an incredibly tall mast – so tall that it is in space! Its dish aerial broadcasts the signals over a very wide area. Receiving dishes on the ground collect and focus the signals and feed them to the television set. The satellite orbits at a speed that corresponds to the earth's rotation, so that it hangs in the same spot in the sky.

Satellite in geostationary orbit

Dish focuses signals

Transmitting dish

Receiver

Receiving dish

24 frames per second

Final images on screen

Computer

Titles and credits text

Keyboard input

GRAND PRIX CIRCUIT

SUSPENSION, BRAKES AND STEERING

2

RACING CAR

1

GASOLINE ENGINE

3

DIFFERENTIAL

6

TRANSMISSION

4

5 **ENGINE LAYOUTS**

Air intake

Rear wing

Disc brakes

Gearbox

Engine

Cooling radiators

1 RACING CAR

Formula One racing cars are at the forefront of automobile design and technology. Even with engines limited to a capacity of 1500 cc (cubic centimeters), they produce up to 10 times the power of a standard family car engine of about 2000 cc! At speeds of 185 miles per hour on a straight track, aerodynamic design is very important. Air passing over the airfoils, or wings, creates downward thrust. This presses the car down, keeping its tires firmly in contact with the track to minimize wheel spins and skids. The driver sits back in an almost supine position for extra streamlining.

SUSPENSION, BRAKES AND STEERING

The car's suspension system helps to absorb bumps and hollows in the road, giving a smoother ride. It also allows the car body to tilt slightly as it goes around a bend, for better cornering. A typical suspension unit has both a coil spring and a hydraulic shock unit, where fluid moves into and out of the cylinder and "dampens" the vibrations. Formula One cars and other performance cars have disc brakes. Stationary brake pads attached to the chassis press on a disc that revolves with the road wheel. The disc brake is more effective and stays cooler than the drum brake, in which curved brake shoes press outward onto the inside of a revolving drum attached to the road wheel. Both types work by hydraulic pressure (page 53). In rack-and-pinion steering, the steering wheel turns a shaft that ends in a small pinion gear. This meshes with the rack, which is a "straightened" gear wheel. As the pinion rotates it makes the rack slide along, moving levers that turn the road wheels.

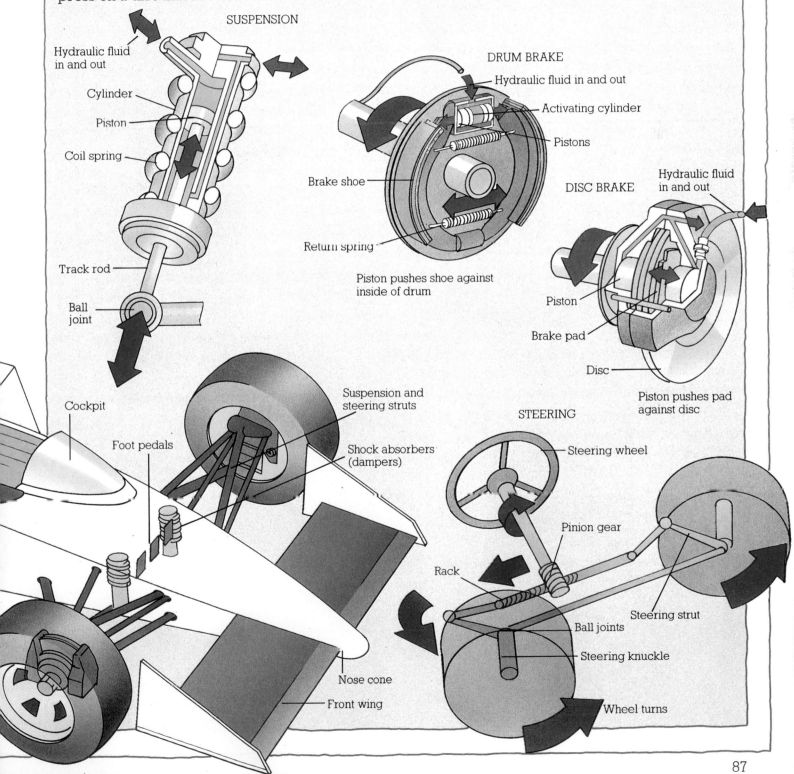

SUSPENSION

Hydraulic fluid in and out

Cylinder

Piston

Coil spring

Track rod

Ball joint

DRUM BRAKE

Hydraulic fluid in and out

Activating cylinder

Pistons

Brake shoe

Return spring

Piston pushes shoe against inside of drum

DISC BRAKE

Hydraulic fluid in and out

Piston

Brake pad

Disc

Piston pushes pad against disc

Cockpit

Foot pedals

Suspension and steering struts

Shock absorbers (dampers)

STEERING

Steering wheel

Pinion gear

Rack

Steering strut

Ball joints

Steering knuckle

Nose cone

Front wing

Wheel turns

GASOLINE ENGINE

In the type of internal combustion engine that runs on gas the energy comes from chemical substances in the gasoline, which has been purified from crude petroleum (page 107). Inside each cylinder of the engine, a mixture of gasoline vapors and air is ignited by an electrically produced spark (*opposite*). This produces a mini-explosion, or combustion, which forces the piston down inside the cylinder. The piston is linked to a crankshaft that transforms an oscillating (back-and-forth) movement into a rotary one. Most ordinary car engines have four or six cylinders. As each piston moves inside its cylinder, from its lowest to its highest position, it pushes or *displaces* a certain volume of air from the cylinder. Add together these displacement volumes for all the cylinders in the engine, and this gives the capacity for the engine, usually measured in cubic centimeters (cc). If each piston in a four-cylinder engine displaces 500 cc, then the capacity of the engine is $4 \times 500 = 2000$ cc (two quarts).

The carburetor mixes air with fuel to give the correct explosive mixture for the cylinder. Each piston on its *induction* stroke (*opposite*) sucks in air from the atmosphere. The air flows through a narrowed part of the carburetor, the *venturi*, where it speeds up and sucks in fuel from the fuel pipe. A tapered needle moves up or down inside a tube to control the amount of fuel entering the carburetor.

Piston

CARBURETOR

Mixture of air and fuel to cylinders

Throttle valve

Needle valve

Fuel line

Air

Fuel pump

Starter motor

Distributor

Oil filter

Air filter

Exhaust valv

Carburetor

Inlet valve

Piston

Crankcase

After combustion, exhaust gases rushing from the cylinder represent energy going to waste. The turbocharger is a turbine-based device (page 71) spun by these rushing gases. It compresses air and forces extra air/fuel mixture into the cylinders, which increases the power from each combustion explosion.

Exhausts from turbine

Compressed air to cylinder

Turbine blades

Turbine casing

AIR IN

Turbine shaft

EXHAUST GASES IN

In the diesel type of internal combustion engine the extremely high pressure inside the cylinder raises the temperature of the air/fuel mixture to exploding point. In a gas engine, a spark plug makes an electrically generated spark which sets fire to the mixture. As the engine turns, cams open and close valves in the top of the cylinder. These work in the correct sequence to let in the air/fuel mixture, contain it during combustion, and then let out the waste gases afterward.

Fuel injector

Inlet valve

Spark plug

Terminal insulator

Central electrode

Exhaust valve

Cylinder

Screw seating

Earth electrode

Piston

Spark

Exhaust manifold

Cooling fan

Fan belt

The family car's gasoline engine is four-stroke. Each piston repeatedly goes through a cycle that lasts four strokes: down, up, down, up. First is the down stroke of *induction*, when air/fuel mixture is drawn into the cylinder. Second is *compression* as the mixture is squeezed, raising its temperature. Third is *ignition*, when the mixture is exploded by a spark. Fourth is *exhaust*, as waste gases from the explosion are pushed out. Some smaller engines are two-stroke (*right, below*).

Induction

Compression

Ignition (second turn)

Exhaust (second turn)

FOUR-STROKE CYCLE

TWO-STROKE CYCLE

Induction

Compression

Ignition

Exhaust

4

TRANSMISSION

There are at least four mechanical devices involved in changing the turning motion of the car's engine to its road wheels: clutch, gearbox, drive shaft and final drives. Together, these are called the transmission.

All the time the engine is running, the crankshaft is turning – but the car may be standing still in neutral or cruising along in top gear. The clutch disconnects the engine's spinning crankshaft from the gearbox when changing gears. When the clutch is engaged or ''in'' (pedal up), the plates press together and transfer the turning motion to the gears. The

clutch is disengaged or ''out'' (pedal pressed) when the two plates are pulled slightly apart. Inside the gearbox, a system of shafts and gear wheels slide back and forth to change gears. In first gear, the engine turns the road wheels slowly but with much *torque* (turning force). In top gear, for the same engine speed, the wheels turn much faster but with less torque.

In cars that have automatic transmission (*bottom*), the gears change themselves according to the speed of the engine and the turning power needed.

Clutch pedal pressed — MANUAL TRANSMISSION — CLUTCH OUT
Crankshaft from engine
Diaphragm flattened
Flywheel
Clutch plates separated

Clutch pedal released — CLUTCH IN
Diaphragm flexed
Clutch plates pressed together

NEUTRAL

FIRST GEAR
Transmission path

AUTOMATIC TRANSMISSION
Planetary gears
Brake bands
Clutch plates
Torque converter
Drive to road wheels
Flywheel
Governor
Annulus
Input shaft
Drive from engine

5 ENGINE LAYOUTS

A car's stability, handling and maneuverability depend partly on how the weight of the various parts is spread among the four road wheels. Particularly important is the position of the heaviest component, the engine. Also important is whether the engine drives the front or rear wheels, or all four wheels together. A Formula One racing car has a mid-mounted, in-line engine that drives the rear wheels. Several other layouts, or *configurations*, are shown here. The mid-engined layout provides good weight distribution. However, in a family car it would take up much of the space that is normally set aside for luggage, in the trunk. Four-wheel drive is best for soft, bumpy or otherwise difficult terrain.

Front-wheel drive, transverse engine

Rear-wheel drive, in-line engine

Rear-wheel drive, rear-mounted engine

Four-wheel drive from front-mounted engine

6 DIFFERENTIAL

As a car rounds a corner, the wheels on the outside of the bend travel farther than those on the inside (*far right*). If the wheels are not driven by the engine, each can rotate independently at its own speed. But wheels driven by the engine would skip and skid if they rotated at the same speed. The differential lets the wheels turn at different speeds. The pinion on the drive shaft transmits power to the ring gear. This turns two *bevel* gears, which mesh with bevel gears on the half-shafts. When the inner road wheel slows down, the outer one speeds up; the ring gear turns at the average speed.

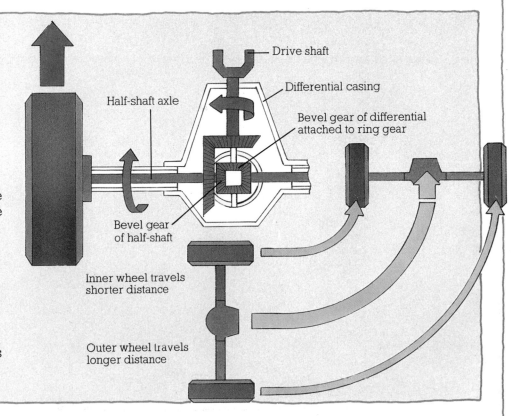

Drive shaft

Differential casing

Half-shaft axle

Bevel gear of differential attached to ring gear

Bevel gear of half-shaft

Inner wheel travels shorter distance

Outer wheel travels longer distance

THE SPORTS CENTER

SAILING
6

SOCCER BALL
5

BOUNCING
8

SHOOTING
7

3
BAR CODE

2
TURNSTILE

4
LCD
STOPWATCH

1
LIGHT METER

1 LIGHT METER

In outdoor games such as tennis and baseball, players should be able to see the ball clearly! When the sky is overcast, or toward dusk, the light may be too dim for good play. In the light meter, a photoresistor changes its resistance to electricity according to how much light falls on it. The result is shown by a small needle and dial or a liquid crystal display (LCD).

LIGHT
Photoresistor
Dial
Pointer
Switch
Battery
Milliammeter

2 TURNSTILE

This simple, robust machine is a ratchet. The teeth on the cog wheel slope in one direction. The wheel can turn one way, since the single tooth or "dog" on the sprung bar is pushed aside smoothly by the sloping part of each tooth on the wheel. But try to turn the wheel the other way, and the dog jams against the first tooth and prevents the wheel from rotating.

Axle
Sloped cogs
Rotating wheel
Hinged dog

3 BAR CODE

Many items are now labeled with a bar code, a series of thick and thin black lines. They carry encoded information – from the membership number of a sports club, to the price and stock number of a box of cookies in a supermarket. The code is scanned by a beam, and the light pulses are turned into electrical signals which are fed into a computer for processing.

Bar code on membership card
Holographic disk
Semi-silvered mirror
Beam splitter
Infrared detector
Infrared beam
Coded signals to computer

4 LCD STOPWATCH

Each segment of a liquid crystal display consists of many liquid crystals sandwiched between two electrodes. The crystals can flow like a liquid. When electricity passes between the electrodes, it twists the crystals so that they do not transmit polarized light; that segment then appears black. Place the lenses of two polarized sunglasses together and twist them for the same effect.

Battery
Liquid crystal
Segments of display set
Displayed letter or number

5 SOCCER BALL

An old-fashioned soccer ball has leather panels stitched together to leave a slitlike opening for the inflatable bladder inside. The opening is then laced up like a shoe. However, this causes problems because of unequal weight distribution, which makes the ball wobble as it spins. It can also be uncomfortable for a player who heads the ball on the laced-up part! Most balls today have leather panels that are shaped in groups to form parts of a sphere. They are stitched together inside out. Before the last seam is sewn, the ball is turned inside in and the inflatable bladder is inserted. The finished ball is perfectly round and well-balanced.

6 SAILING

Sail-based sports such as yachting and windsurfing rely on the energy of the wind to push on the broad surface of the sail, which is attached to the craft. Being blown along in the direction of the wind is known as *running (near right)*. In order to travel across the wind, the craft and sail are set at angles as shown for *reaching (far right)*. The resistance of the craft to being pushed sideways combines with the direction of the wind on the sail, to make the craft travel forward. The sailor can move into the wind by *beating*, to the left and right alternately, on a zigzag course into the wind (*middle right*).

RUNNING (DOWNWIND)

Direction of movement

Sail

Mast

Wind

Boom

Board

BEATING (INTO WIND)

Wind

Direction of moveme

Forc
from

Heeling forc

7 SHOOTING

A basic law of physics says: "Every action has an equal and opposite reaction." When the powder in a shell casing explodes, it pushes the bullet one way – out of the barrel. The gun reacts by moving the other way, which is called the recoil.

Reaction (gun recoils)

Action (shell is fired)

Shell casing

Shell

8 BOUNCING

As a rubber ball falls against the ground, it becomes squashed and stores energy – in a similar, but opposite, way to a stretched elastic band. The ball comes to a sudden halt. The energy is released as the elastic material springs back into shape and propels the ball upward again.

Ball falls

Ball reforms

Ball deforms

Elastic material of ball

Bounce

REACHING (ACROSS WIND)

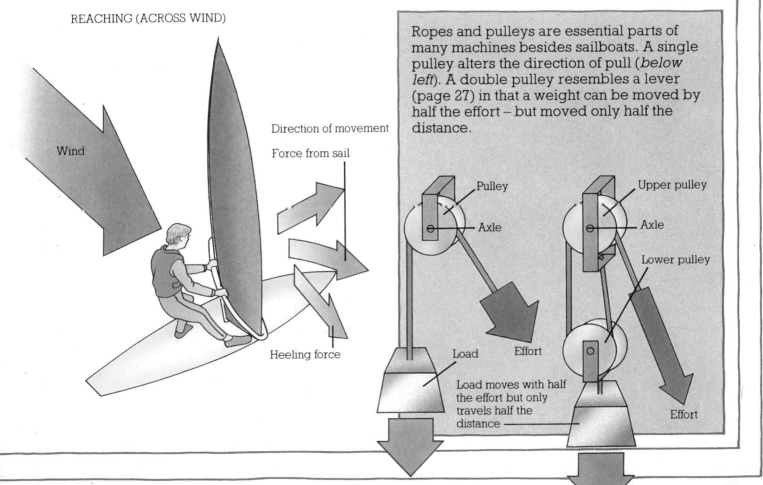

Wind

Direction of movement

Force from sail

Heeling force

Ropes and pulleys are essential parts of many machines besides sailboats. A single pulley alters the direction of pull (*below left*). A double pulley resembles a lever (page 27) in that a weight can be moved by half the effort – but moved only half the distance.

Pulley

Axle

Load

Effort

Upper pulley

Axle

Lower pulley

Effort

Load moves with half the effort but only travels half the distance

95

PRODUCTION LINE

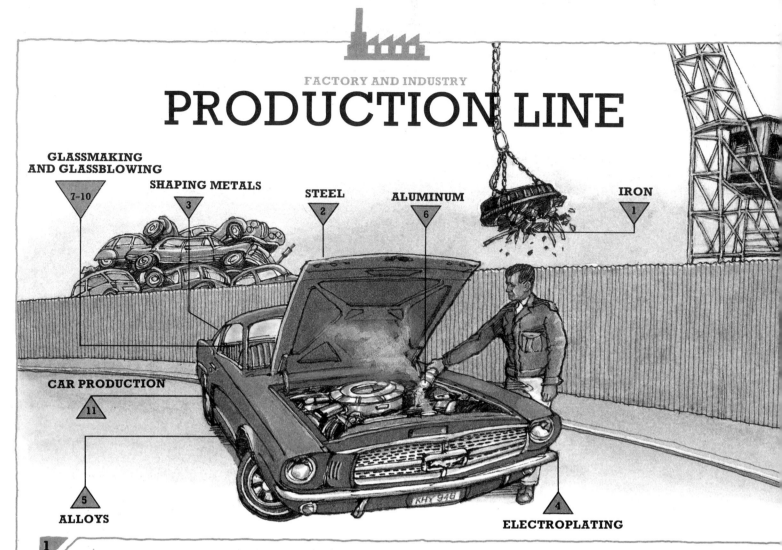

GLASSMAKING
AND GLASSBLOWING
7-10

SHAPING METALS
3

STEEL
2

ALUMINUM
6

IRON
1

CAR PRODUCTION
11

ALLOYS
5

ELECTROPLATING
4

1 IRON

Pure metals are rarely found in nature, although lumps of pure iron sometimes reach the earth in meteorites. Instead, metals are usually found combined chemically with other substances, such as metal ores. Iron was one of the first metals to be purified from its ore, over 3500 years ago. A modern blast furnace makes up to 10,000 tons of iron daily. In the furnace, preheated air is blasted through a mixture of iron oxide ore, limestone and a fuel such as coke. As the coke burns it forms the gas carbon monoxide. This combines chemically with the iron oxide to give carbon dioxide and iron, while the limestone soaks up other impurities to create the slag. The resulting iron, still not completely pure, is known as pig iron. It is further refined to wrought iron, cast iron, steel and other forms.

Limestone

Coal

Coke furnace

Iron ore

Crushing mills

Blending hopper

Blended ingredients

2 STEEL

Molten iron from the blast furnace is relatively impure, containing 5 percent or more of carbon. In the converter it is changed into purer forms known as steel. There are many kinds of steel, made by different processes. In the basic oxygen process (*right*), molten pig iron is poured onto scrap in a huge vessel. A lance about six feet above the surface blows high-pressure oxygen over the molten metal bath for about 20 minutes. The oxygen combines with the carbon and removes it from the metal. Steels are irons that contain less than 1.7 percent of carbon. Tiny amounts of other substances may be added such as manganese, nickel and chromium.

Molten pig iron

Oxygen

Lime

Lance (cooled tube)

Converter

Lime combines with impurities

Steel is poured off

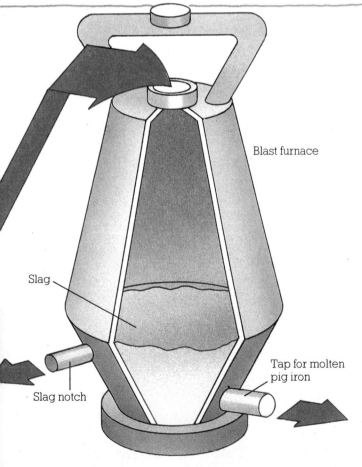

Blast furnace

Slag

Slag notch

Tap for molten pig iron

3 SHAPING METALS

We value metals such as iron and steel for their toughness. This same property makes them difficult to shape. If the metal is heated above its melting point, so that it turns into a liquid, it can be molded or formed in a variety of ways. Iron's melting point is 2795°F. Some metals, like copper, are *ductile*, which means they can be squeezed or drawn out when cold into different shapes (like thin wires) yet still keep their strength.

Casting

Forging

Rolling

Drawing

Extruding

Machining

4 ELECTROPLATING

When a substance dissolves in a liquid to form a solution, its component parts float freely as electrically charged particles called *ions*. For example, a solution of common salt, or sodium chloride, forms sodium and chlorine ions. Pass an electric current through the solution between two electrodes and the ions are attracted to the electrode of the opposite charge, in the same way that unlike poles of magnets attract. Electroplating employs an electric current to coat one electrode – the item to be plated – with a substance such as a metal. The metal exists in the form of ions floating about in solution. Metal ions are positively charged, so they gather on the negative electrode, known as the cathode.

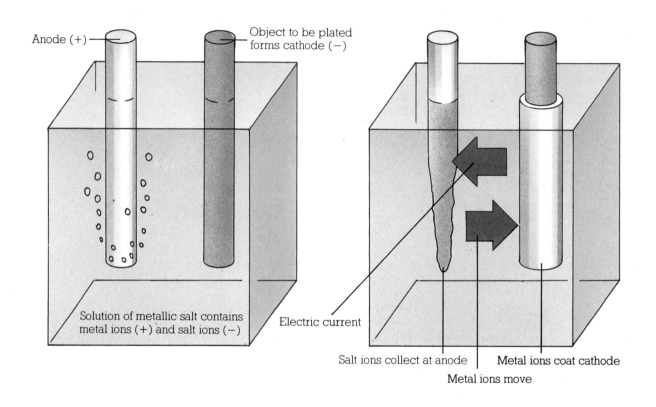

Anode (+)

Object to be plated forms cathode (−)

Solution of metallic salt contains metal ions (+) and salt ions (−)

Electric current

Salt ions collect at anode

Metal ions coat cathode

Metal ions move

5 ALLOYS

An alloy is a mixture of metals or a mixture of a metal and another substance. *Bronze* is an alloy of copper and tin. *Steel* is an alloy of iron and carbon. *Stainless steel* is an alloy of steel with nickel and chromium. One familiar alloy is silver combined with the liquid metal mercury, which forms the amalgam of tooth fillings. Titanium-steel alloys are used for their lightness and strength in planes and spacecraft. Nickel-cobalt "superalloys" are used in jet-engine turbine blades (page 47) to withstand temperatures of over 1800°F. At the other end of the scale, alloys of metals such as lead, bismuth and cadmium melt at temperatures as low as 122°F and are used in fire alarms (page 61).

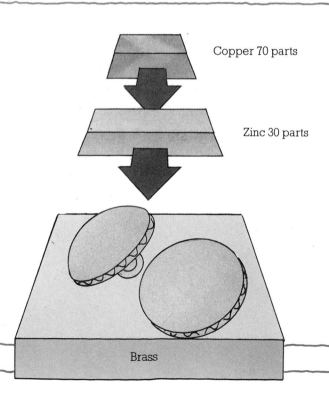

Copper 70 parts

Zinc 30 parts

Brass

ALUMINUM

6

Aluminum, an extremely light metal, is also very abundant – it makes up one-twelfth of the earth's crust. Its ores are mainly *bauxites*, in which aluminum is combined with oxygen, sand, iron, titanium and other substances. The bauxite is first refined into alumina, a purer form of aluminum oxide, by the Bayer process. The alumina is then separated into aluminum and oxygen by *electrolysis* (*see also electroplating, opposite*). This is done at almost

1835°F in a bath of molten cryolite, another substance containing aluminum, as well as sodium and fluorine.

An electric current passes through the alumina between two electrodes – the carbon rods (positive anodes) above, and the carbon linings (negative cathodes) of the reduction pots. The electric current splits the aluminum and oxygen; the positive aluminum gathers around the cathodes and is siphoned off.

Bauxite ore —— Hopper

Alumina

Reduction pot

Carbon anodes (+)

Cryolite electrolysis bath

Aluminum ions (+)

Carbon lining cathode (−)

Molten aluminum is siphoned off

Oxygen ions (−)

Molten aluminum

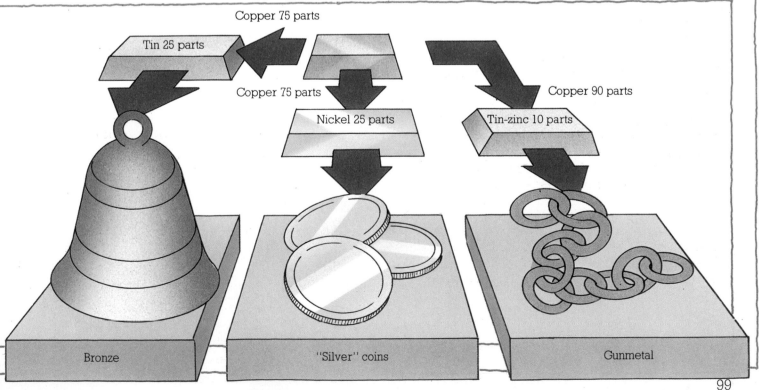

Copper 75 parts

Tin 25 parts

Copper 75 parts

Nickel 25 parts

Copper 90 parts

Tin-zinc 10 parts

Bronze

"Silver" coins

Gunmetal

7

Potash
Limestone
Cullet (waste glass)

Regeneration furnace

Bath of molten tin

Sand (silica)

Blending hopper

Thin layer of molten glass floats on molten tin in oxygen-free environment

Annealing lehr (cooling unit)

GLASSMAKING

Glass has been made for over 3500 years. It is produced by heating raw materials, mainly sand (silica), soda or potash, and limestone to temperatures of about 2370°F in a furnace. There are small amounts of other additives, such as alumina and magnesia. The float glass process was developed by Alistair Pilkington in the 1950s to make sheets of flat glass. Molten glass from the furnace is floated over a bath of molten tin metal, and the smooth top of the liquid metal gives the glass an extremely smooth, shiny surface. The sheet glass then cools and hardens in the *annealing lehr*.

8

GLASSBLOWING

Typical soda glass is made chiefly from silica (72 percent), soda or sodium oxide (15 percent) and lime (5 percent). It softens at around 1292°F and can then be blown into a hollow shape, by forcing air into a molten blob, or gob, of the glass. The glassblower reheats, reblows, twirls and shapes the glass to produce the finished object. Machines make light bulbs from ribbons of glass.

Molten glass from furnace

Blowpipe

Air blown into glass
Hollow sphere

Shaping bench
Glass twirled on blowp

Pre

9 SAFETY GLASS

Glass can be strengthened enormously by sandwiching a wire mesh between two sheets. This type of glass is used for windows and screens that do not have to be perfectly transparent but that may allow a view or let in daylight while remaining very strong.

Wire reinforcing mesh

Hot sheet glass

Hot sheet glass

Rollers

Sheet glass to cutting shop

Conveyor rollers

10 GLASS CONTAINERS

Bottles, jars and similar glass containers are blown by the thousands on large automatic machines. One method is shown below. In another version a gob of glass is put into a blank mold and pressed into a preliminary tube shape, the *parison*, by a metal plunger. The parison is then put into a bigger blow mold and is blown by compressed air into the finished bottle or jar shape. Glass is used for containers because it is smooth-surfaced, easily cleaned, does not react with most contents – and you can see what's inside.

Molten glass

Air in

Blow mold (in parts)

Finished bottle cools

Air in

Air in

Trimming

Finishing

Cooling

...s glass flexible

11 CAR PRODUCTION

In 1913, Henry Ford began mass-producing his Ford Model T cars using a moving assembly line. His basic process is still used today. The car moves along a track, rails or conveyor and is assembled part by part. A summary of the whole procedure is shown below. In practice, the engines may be made in one factory while the chassis is produced in another and the body is pressed and painted in the body shop at another site. These subassemblies are then transported to the main production line for final assembly. The work is checked at each stage by quality control staff. Every so often the production line is halted and altered to produce a different version of the basic car, depending on what buyers have ordered or how fashions change. For example, the same body may be fitted with a smaller capacity engine for better fuel economy.

Sheet metal press

Robot welders join sheets

Metal is pressed into shape

Body is dipped in primer and undercoat tanks

Robot sprayers add final coats of paint

The repetitive movements on the production line – fitting the same part time after time – are ideal work for computer-controlled robots. In the direct training method, a skilled worker first "teaches" the computer the correct movements. These are stored in the computer memory, and copied by the hydraulic robot arm at the desired speed.

DIRECT TRAINING

Hydraulic arms

Operator carries out movements

In the fully automated factory, materials and parts and subassemblies can be transported from place to place by autocarriers. The vehicle follows a guide wire laid in the floor. Signals pass from operator to vehicle along another wire, telling the carrier which route to take. Signals also pass from vehicle to operator along a third wire, letting the operator keep track of the carrier's position. The operator's computer is programmed to send the autocarrier on a standard route.

Concentrator

Computer

Operator's desk and terminal

Guide and pick-up wires buried in factory floor

Autocarrier

Transmitter antenna

Guide antenna

Receiver antenna

Treated body on conveyor

Autocarrier delivers mechanics and chassis by following guide wire

Marriage of body and chassis

Loom of electrical wiring

Doors

Windows

Interior fixtures

Mechanics and chassis assembled
(engine, transmission, drive shaft, suspension and brakes)

Wheels and tires

Postassembling check

TEXTILES

NATURAL FIBERS

1

ARTIFICIAL FIBERS

3

WEAVING

4

SPINNING

2

1

NATURAL FIBERS

Natural fibers are those produced by animals and plants, such as wool from sheep and goats, and cotton from the fluffy seed heads of cotton plants. Freshly harvested cotton bolls contain the cotton fibers, called *lint*, as well as seeds, leaves and other smaller fibers. In the cotton gin, the fibers are dried and pulled by revolving teeth through small gratings to remove the seeds and other debris. The fibers are then ready to be spun (*above right*). Silk is another natural fiber. It comes from the silkworm – the caterpillar of the silkworm moth. As the caterpillar changes into a chrysalis, it spins a cocoon of silken threads around itself. Each cocoon may contain up to 1600 yards of extremely thin silk filament.

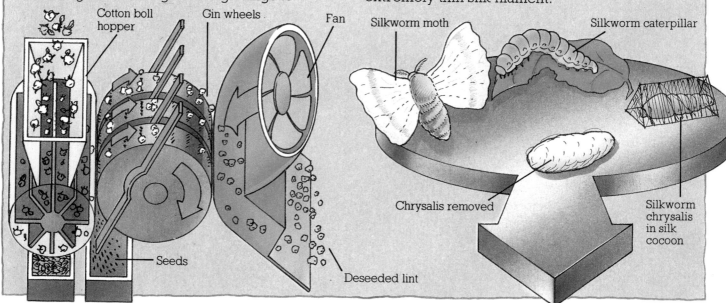

Cotton boll hopper

Gin wheels

Fan

Seeds

Deseeded lint

Silkworm moth

Silkworm caterpillar

Chrysalis removed

Silkworm chrysalis in silk cocoon

2 ▸ SPINNING

At the start of the spinning process, the mat of cotton fibers, known as the lap, travels through teasing wires in a carding machine to produce loose bundles of fibers called slivers (*below left*). The slivers are teased and pulled out by rollers rotating at different rates (*below center*) and wound onto reels or bobbins. The slivers are then thinned even further and spun into cotton yarn that is wound on another bobbin, ready for weaving or knitting into cotton cloth.

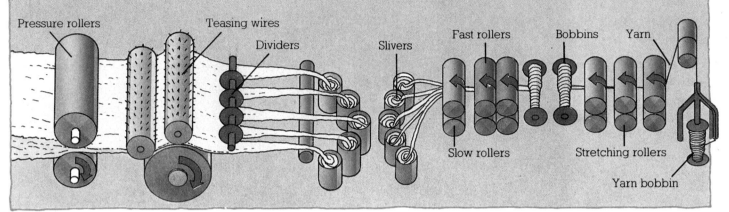

Pressure rollers · Teasing wires · Dividers · Slivers · Fast rollers · Bobbins · Yarn · Slow rollers · Stretching rollers · Yarn bobbin

3 ▸ ARTIFICIAL FIBERS

Chemicals are used to make artificial or synthetic fibers such as nylon, polyester and acrylic. A common type, nylon 66, is made from hexamethylene diamine and adipic acid. The molecules *polymerize*, which means they link together in enormously long chains that give the material its strength and flexibility. In one technique, the raw chemicals are melted, extruded into long filaments, cooled and spun together.

Nylon polymer chips · Steam · Cooling air · Spinneret · Heater · Cooled fiber

4 ▸ WEAVING

In a woven fabric the yarns run in a crisscross fashion, alternately over and under each other. The warp yarns are the ones already arranged in place along the weaving loom. Their ends are wound onto the warp beam. The weft or filler yarn is then passed back and forth between the alternating sets of warps, which are moved up and down on harness beams. Each harness beam moves every other warp yarn. The weft yarn unwinds from the shuttle.

Warp beam · Shuttle · Up · Down · Woven cloth · Down · Up

THE REFINERY

REFINING NATURAL GAS

1

REFINING NATURAL GAS

Natural gas collects in pockets within the earth's crust and is obtained by drilling, in a similar way as for oil (page 62). It is about nine-tenths methane, a hydrocarbon (combination of hydrogen and carbon) with the chemical formula CH_4. But there are usually other hydrocarbon gases mixed with it, such as ethane (C_2H_6), propane (C_3H_8), and butane (C_4H_{10}). Each of these is suitable as a fuel or raw material in its own right. At the refinery, the gases are separated by *fractionation*. Each gas has a different boiling point, and fractionation relies on changes in temperature and pressure to tap off each gas in turn. Liquefied petroleum gas is made from crude petroleum (*opposite*) or by refining from natural gas. It contains greater proportions of propane and butane than natural gas, and it turns into a liquid more easily, making it more suitable for transport by tanker.

Natural gas

Extraction plant

Fractionation plant

Slug catcher

Freezing unit

Liquefied natural gas tanker

REFINING PETROLEUM

2

REFINING PETROLEUM

Crude oil or petroleum, straight from the well (page 63), is a complicated mixture of many different substances. Most are hydrocarbons. Nitrogen and sulfur compounds are present in varying amounts. At the oil refinery, the raw petroleum is separated into its various ingredients by the process of "cracking." The crude oil is heated and passes into a fractionation tower. Different levels of the tower are at different temperatures, and the various petroleum products, or "fractions," condense at each level. The heaviest fractions stay near the bottom, while the lighter ones such as gasoline form toward the top.

Petroleum gases

Gasoline

Kerosene

Distillation tray

Distillate   Vapors

Diesel oils

Fractionation tower

Lubricating oils

Ethane

Pressurization units

Propane

Fuel oils

Butane

Crude oil

Natural gasoline

Bitumen, asphalt, tars, waxes

INSIDE YOUR BODY

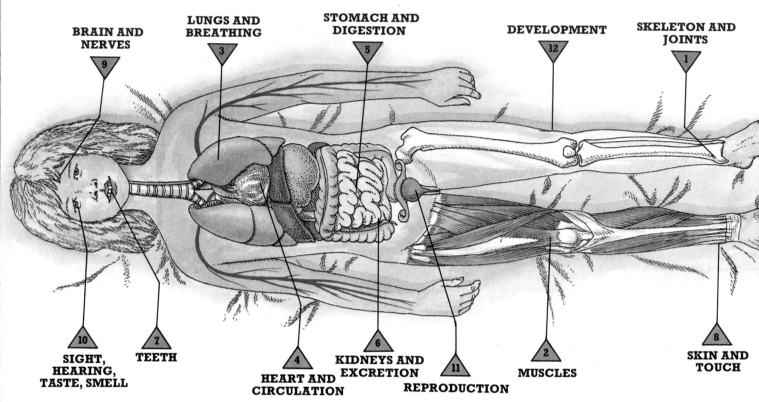

BRAIN AND NERVES 9

LUNGS AND BREATHING 3

STOMACH AND DIGESTION 5

DEVELOPMENT 12

SKELETON AND JOINTS 1

SIGHT, HEARING, TASTE, SMELL 10

TEETH 7

HEART AND CIRCULATION 4

KIDNEYS AND EXCRETION 6

REPRODUCTION 11

MUSCLES 2

SKIN AND TOUCH 8

---

1 **SKELETON AND JOINTS**

The human body has a framework of about 208 rigid bones, which together make up its skeleton. Each bone is hard and strong, composed chiefly of calcium, phosphate, and other minerals and a tough protein known as collagen. Where bones meet, there are joints. Some joints, like those between the skull bones, are fixed and do not allow movement. Other joints let the bones move in relation to each other. The largest single bone is the femur (the thigh bone), and the biggest single joint is the knee. The smallest joints are between the smallest bones, in the ear (page 112).

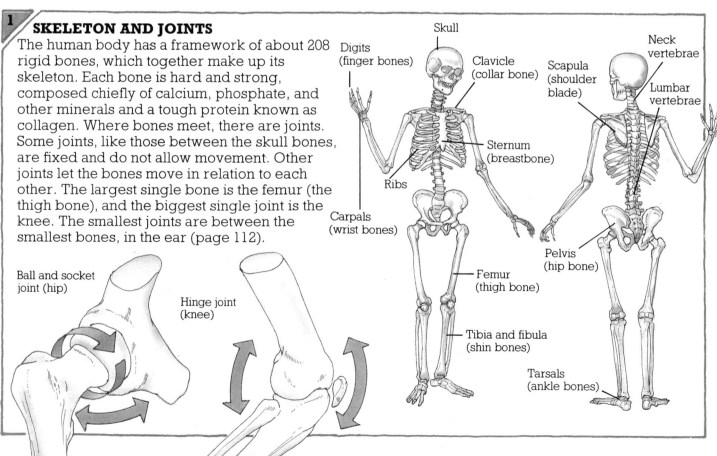

Ball and socket joint (hip)

Hinge joint (knee)

Skull

Digits (finger bones)

Clavicle (collar bone)

Sternum (breastbone)

Ribs

Carpals (wrist bones)

Femur (thigh bone)

Tibia and fibula (shin bones)

Tarsals (ankle bones)

Neck vertebrae

Scapula (shoulder blade)

Lumbar vertebrae

Pelvis (hip bone)

2 MUSCLES

There are over 600 skeletal muscles in the body. They move the skeleton, and they are under conscious control, so you can will them to move when you wish. Many other muscles are in the digestive system (page 110), heart and other internal organs, but these work mainly automatically. A muscle can pull but not push. Most skeletal muscles are arranged in pairs. One pulls the bone one way, and the other pulls it back.

Biceps relaxed

Triceps contracted

Biceps contracted

Triceps relaxed

3 LUNGS AND BREATHING

The lungs, trachea (windpipe), throat and nose make up the body's respiratory, or breathing, system. To breathe in, a series of muscles pushes the ribs outward while the diaphragm muscle becomes flat and pulls the bases of the lungs downward. This makes the lungs bigger, and they draw in air. To breathe out, the various muscles relax. The elastic lung tissue springs back, returning the lungs to their smaller size and pushing out the air.

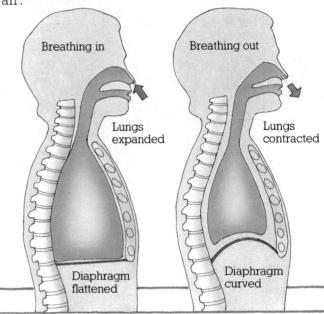

Breathing in

Breathing out

Lungs expanded

Lungs contracted

Diaphragm flattened

Diaphragm curved

4 HEART AND CIRCULATION

In the lungs, blood absorbs oxygen from the air. The blood then flows to the heart, which pumps it around the body, to deliver its oxygen to all body parts. In one heartbeat, blood is first drawn into the two upper chambers, the atria (1). It then flows through nonreturn valves into the lower chambers, the ventricles (2). These squeeze powerfully to push the blood out through the blood vessels, closing the valves to the atria (3). As the ventricles expand again, valves into the main vessels close to prevent blood from flowing back into them (4).

Venae cavae (main veins) from body

Pulmonary artery to lungs

Right atrium

Aorta (main artery) to body

Right ventricle

Pulmonary vein from lungs

Left atrium

Left ventricle

1

2

3

4

5 STOMACH AND DIGESTION

Like any mechanism, the body needs fuel. It obtains this from food. Digestion is the process of breaking down food into pieces small enough to be absorbed through the wall of the small intestine into the blood. The teeth and the stomach chew and mash the food physically, while the stomach and the pancreas make powerful digestive juices that attack the food chemically. Food moves through the digestive system by the muscle-powered process of peristalsis. Leftover bits, together with rubbed-off parts of the stomach and intestines, are stored in the large intestine before disposal.

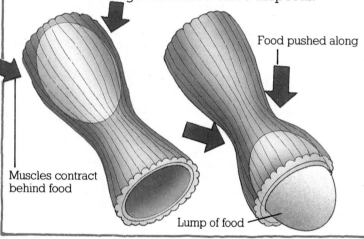

Food pushed along

Muscles contract behind food

Lump of food

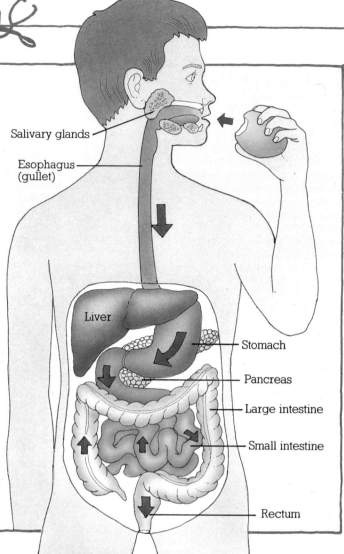

Salivary glands
Esophagus (gullet)
Liver
Stomach
Pancreas
Large intestine
Small intestine
Rectum

6 KIDNEYS AND EXCRETION

The hundreds of chemical processes inside the body make various unwanted substances. The blood collects them. As it flows through the kidneys, more than a million microscopic filtering units in each kidney clean the blood. The wastes form a fluid, urine. This trickles down tubes, or ureters, and is stored in the bladder.

Filtered blood returns to heart

Blood carrying wastes

Kidney filters blood to produce urine

Urine flows down ureters

Urine expelled through urethra

Urine stored in bladder

7 TEETH

The whitish enamel of a tooth is the hardest substance in the body. Inside, the tooth's living center contains blood vessels and nerves. Its roots are fixed into the jaw bone by slightly flexible ligaments, which absorb some of the shocks and jars of biting. A child has a set of 20 teeth, and an adult has 32. The teeth at the front (incisors) are chisel-shaped for biting; those at the back (molars) are flattened for crushing.

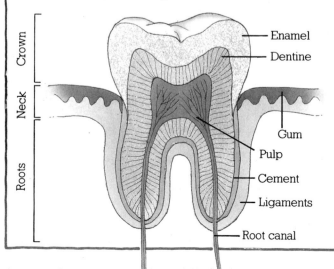

Crown
Neck
Roots

Enamel
Dentine
Gum
Pulp
Cement
Ligaments
Root canal

8 SKIN AND TOUCH

Under a microscope, skin reveals two main layers. The outer layer is the epidermis, the inner one is the dermis. The epidermis continually replaces itself as its surface is rubbed off and worn away by the body's movements and friction. At the base of the epidermis, cells are continually multiplying. They pass up through the various layers within the epidermis, becoming flatter and harder, and they eventually die. They reach the surface after about four weeks, where they are soon rubbed off. The dermis contains blood vessels, tough fibers of the protein collagen, and nerve endings of various kinds that detect changes in temperature, light touch, heavier pressure, and pain.

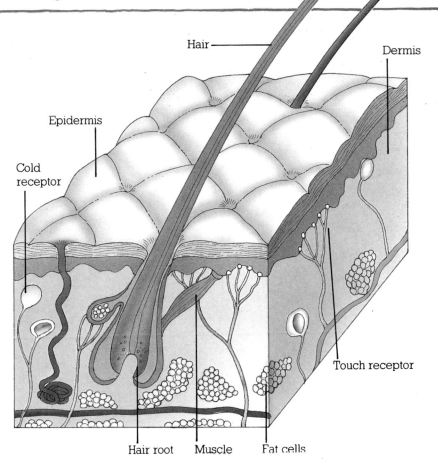

Hair — Dermis
Epidermis
Cold receptor
Touch receptor
Hair root   Muscle   Fat cells

9 BRAIN AND NERVES

The brain is made up of about 10 billion nerve cells, or neurons, connected into one vast network. Nerve signals flash around the network in the form of tiny pulses of electricity. Nerves link the brain to all parts of the body. They carry signals to the brain from the sense organs (skin, eyes, ears, tongue, nose) and signals from the brain to muscles. Most thinking and remembering takes place in the two large wrinkled lobes, the cerebral hemispheres. The corpus callosum connects the right and left halves of the brain. The pituitary gland, just below the main part of the brain, is the controller of the body's system of chemical messengers, known as the hormonal or endocrine system.

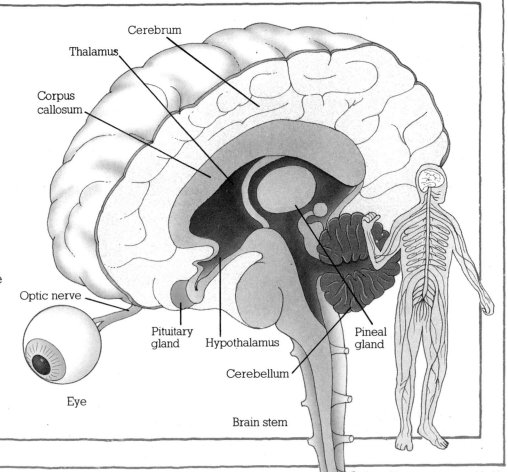

Cerebrum
Thalamus
Corpus callosum
Optic nerve
Pituitary gland
Hypothalamus
Pineal gland
Cerebellum
Eye
Brain stem

10 SIGHT, HEARING, TASTE, SMELL

In the eye, a lens focuses light rays onto a thin layer, the retina, which contains more than 130 million light-sensitive cells. These turn the patterns of light rays into coded nerve signals, which travel to the brain along the optic nerve. The ear changes airborne vibrations – sound waves – into vibrations that pass along three tiny bones, the hammer, anvil, and stirrup. When the vibrations reach the fluid of the inner ear, they rock tiny hairs attached to nerve cells, producing nerve signals that go to the brain. In the tongue, taste buds detect the flavor

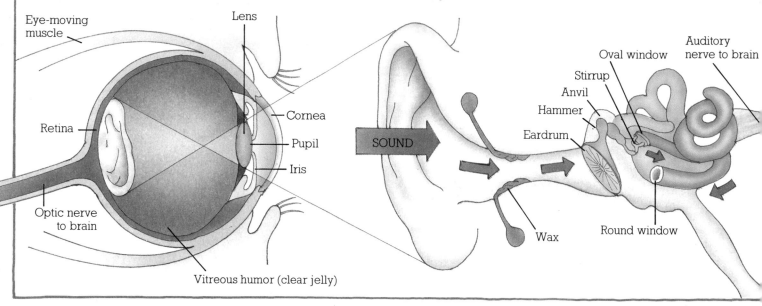

Eye-moving muscle
Lens
Retina
Cornea
Pupil
Iris
Optic nerve to brain
Vitreous humor (clear jelly)

Oval window
Auditory nerve to brain
Stirrup
Anvil
Hammer
Eardrum
SOUND
Wax
Round window

12 DEVELOPMENT

All people begin life as a fertilized egg. The egg, in the woman, is fertilized by the sperm from a man. The egg splits into two, then four, then eight new cells. This continues until there are many millions of cells. Five days after fertilization some cells grow outward from the developing *embryo* and into the wall of the uterus. This forms the placenta, which passes food and oxygen to the embryo. Different cells in the embryo develop into different organs such as the heart and muscles. After nine months the baby is fully formed and is born.

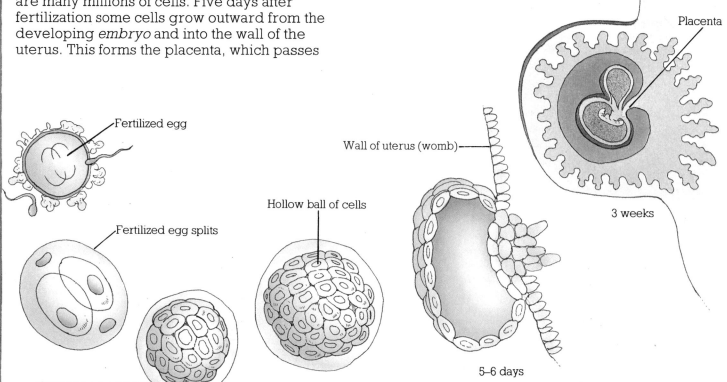

Fertilized egg
Fertilized egg splits
Hollow ball of cells
Wall of uterus (womb)
Placenta
3 weeks
5–6 days

substances in food and drink, converting the chemical reactions into nerve signals – which once again pass to the brain. The nose is the organ of smell. Odors are sensed when chemical molecules combine with receptors in the nose.

Surface of tongue

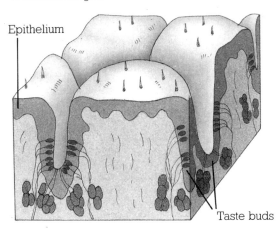

Epithelium

Taste buds

REPRODUCTION

All animals, including humans, begin life as an egg. The human egg is only one-tenth of a millimeter across, and it comes from the woman's ovary. The man's testes make millions of microscopic, tadpole-shaped sperm cells. During sexual intercourse, sperm from the man's penis swim along the woman's vagina and through the uterus, to the egg waiting in the oviduct.

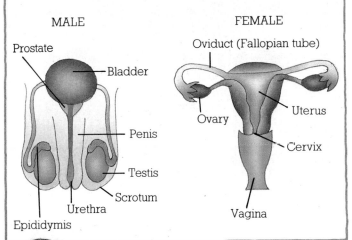

MALE

Prostate
Bladder
Penis
Testis
Scrotum
Urethra
Epididymis

FEMALE

Oviduct (Fallopian tube)
Uterus
Ovary
Cervix
Vagina

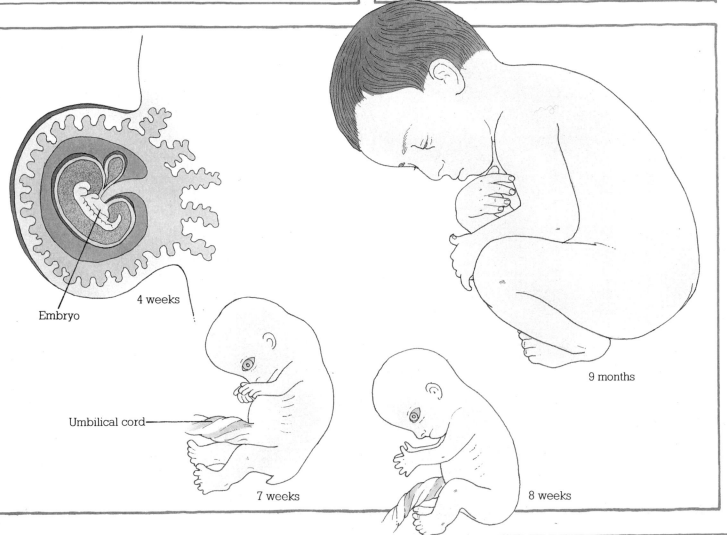

Embryo

4 weeks

Umbilical cord

7 weeks

8 weeks

9 months

THE DOCTOR'S OFFICE

OTOSCOPE AND OPHTHALMOSCOPE 6

HYPODERMIC NEEDLE AND SYRINGE 4

THERMOMETER 3

BODY REFLEXES 1

STETHOSCOPE 5

BLOOD PRESSURE 2

---

1 **BODY REFLEXES**

The brain controls many of the body's actions, but not all of them. A reflex is a sudden, automatic reaction in which nerve messages travel to the spinal cord, pass around a reflex loop, and go out to muscles, without involving the brain. The knee-jerk reflex is a convenient way to check nerves and muscles.

Message to spinal cord

Message passed up spinal cord to brain

Knock on knee

Message back to leg muscle

2 **BLOOD PRESSURE**

Blood pressure is checked with a sphygmomanometer. The cuff is inflated until its air pressure is sufficient to stop blood flowing (temporarily) through an artery in the arm. The doctor listens for blood flow through the stethoscope (*see opposite*). The air pressure pushes liquid mercury around the U-shaped tube.

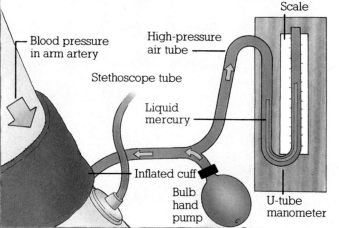

Blood pressure in arm artery

Scale

High-pressure air tube

Stethoscope tube

Liquid mercury

Inflated cuff

Bulb hand pump

U-tube manometer

3 THERMOMETER

Most substances expand when heated, and mercury is no exception. Body heat makes it expand from the bulb up into the stem. The notch stops the mercury in the stem from shrinking back into the bulb, allowing time to take the reading on the scale.

Magnifying side of glass

Notch

Bulb

Scale

Mercury

4 HYPODERMIC NEEDLE AND SYRINGE

Vaccines, drugs and other substances can be injected into the body using a hollow needle. *Hypodermic* means "below the skin." The vaccine is sucked out of its bottle through a self-sealing rubber stopper. Air bubbles must then be removed for they could cause an airlock and prevent blood flow if they got into a blood vessel.

Air

Vaccine

Hypodermic needle

Syringe barrel

5 STETHOSCOPE

This listening device has a thin, flexible diaphragm that vibrates as it picks up sound waves or vibrations. The diaphragm's vibrations create sound waves that funnel up a hollow tube to the earpieces. The stethoscope amplifies sounds from the beating heart, breathing lungs, creaking joints, blood swishing through blood vessels, and food gurgling through intestines.

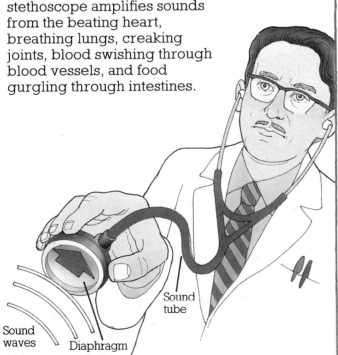

Sound tube

Sound waves

Diaphragm

6 OTOSCOPE AND OPHTHALMOSCOPE

Inside the eye is a convenient place for examining the body's blood vessels, which give an indication of general health. Small vessels show up on the retina, the light-sensitive layer at the back of the eyeball. The ophthalmoscope shines a beam of light into the eye, to illuminate the retina. When looking into the ear with an otoscope, the doctor can see through the partly transparent eardrum to the tiny bones beyond (page 112).

OTOSCOPE

Light bulb

Nozzle

Lens

OPHTHALMOSCOPE

Lens

Light bulb

Eye's own lens magnifies view

Batteries in handle casing

THE OPERATING ROOM

X-RAYS 5

CAT SCANNER 6

ARTIFICIAL IMPLANTS 7

LASER SCALPEL 4

ANESTHETICS 1

HEART-LUNG MACHINE 3

ENDOSCOPE 2

1 ANESTHETICS

An anesthetic is a substance that produces loss of feeling. A general anesthetic does this by making the patient unconscious. Some anesthetics are given by injection into a vein (intravenous injection). Others are given as a gas mixture, which is breathed into the lungs and then absorbed through the lungs into the bloodstream.

Exhalation line

Inhalation line

Lungs

2 ENDOSCOPE

Endoscopes are inserted into the body through an opening, such as the mouth, or through a small cut. Modern versions use a bundle of thin, flexible optical fibers (page 75) that can be steered through the body with a light to illuminate the view and tiny pincers to take a sample, or biopsy, for later analysis. The bronchoscope looks into the lungs, the gastroscope into the stomach, and the cystoscope into the bladder.

Eyepiece

Biopsy forceps control

Control unit and light source

Tip steering control

Air/water jet

Biopsy forceps

Lens

Light beam

Fiberoptic light cable

3 HEART-LUNG MACHINE

The technical name for this device is the cardiopulmonary bypass machine, since it takes over the jobs of both heart and lungs. Blood returning along veins, from the body's organs to the heart, is led out of the body along a tube to a gas-exchange unit. Here carbon dioxide is removed from the blood and oxygen is added – thus doing the lungs' job. The blood then flows through a rotary pump – which does the heart's job – and back into the main arteries. The CP machine is used when surgeons need to operate on the heart, for example, when replacing a diseased heart valve with an artificial one (page 119).

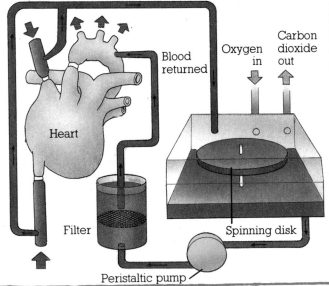

Blood taken from veins

Blood returned

Oxygen in

Carbon dioxide out

Heart

Filter

Spinning disk

Peristaltic pump

Evaporator

Absorber

Valve

Gas mixture

ng bag

Oxygen cylinder

Nitrous oxide cylinder

4 LASER SCALPEL

Laser light is a concentrated form of energy (page 135). It can burn through the body's tissues, in a fashion similar to the metal scalpel blade that cuts through them. But the laser scalpel can be controlled more accurately, producing a thinner, neater cut. Because it is hot it singes and seals the small blood vessels on either side of the cut. This means that there is less bleeding than with a metal scalpel.

Laser source

Fiberoptic cable

Barrel handle

Focusing lens

Laser beam

5 X-RAYS

X-rays are part of the electromagnetic spectrum that includes light rays and radio waves. They pass easily through the body's muscles, intestines and other soft parts. But they cannot travel through the hard parts, such as bones, cartilage and teeth. In a medical X-ray picture, or radiograph, X-rays from a gas-discharge tube shine through the body onto a fluorescent screen and photographic plate. Where rays can pass through, they produce a dark area. Dense parts like bones and metal jewelry show up white.

Electric motor

Tungsten cathode target rotator

X-RAYS

Electron beam

Heated anode

X-rays pass through soft tissues

Photographic plate — Bone and metal absorb X-rays

Processed photographic plate

6 CAT SCANNER

Computerized Axial Tomography involves passing very weak X-rays through the body. The patient lies inside a large rotating drum containing the X-ray source and recording camera. These move around and along the body, taking several pictures from different angles. The pictures are then combined by computer to show a ''slice'' through the body. Like an ordinary X-ray, dense parts of the body show up lighter. The CAT scanner can distinguish between different soft tissues, such as muscles and nerves. The procedure is painless and takes only a few minutes.

Supercooled superconducting magnet in low-loss cryostat

Electrical power

Shim and gradient coils control beam

Computer

Machine scans successive ''slices''

ARTIFICIAL IMPLANTS

7

Many diseased or worn-out parts of the body can now be replaced with artificial substitutes. Medical scientists are continually searching for better, longer lasting materials. These materials should be biologically inert – they should not cause blood to clot on their surfaces, and they should not provoke the body into reacting against them as though they were invaders like germs. Plastics such as Teflon and metals such as stainless steel are often used. As electronic devices become smaller and more sophisticated, they are being used to help parts of the body that rely on electrical nerve messages. For example, the cochlear implant receives sound waves, converts them into electrical signals, and feeds the signals directly to the cochlea, the part of the ear that normally turns vibrations into nerve messages.

Skull plate
Cosmetic false eye
Cochlear implant in ear
False teeth
Artificial larynx
Cardiac pacemaker
Artificial heart valve
Breast implant

Artificial joint

Knee-cap relacement

Plastic artery

ARTIFICIAL HEART VALVE

Valve open

Forward pressure of blood

Position of valve at entrance to aorta

Ball-and-cage valve

Valve closed

ARTIFICIAL HIP JOINT

Plastic socket in hip bone

Head of femur removed

Metal alloy ball at top of femur

COCHLEAR IMPLANT

Transmitter coil

Receiver coil

Electrode transmits signals into cochlea

Microphone

Electrode

HARVEST TIME

MILKING PARLOR 6

GRAIN HANDLING 3

SEED DRILL 8

PLOW 7

CROP SPRAYER 9

COMBINE 2

BALER 4

TRACTOR 5

BEET HARVESTER 1

1 BEET HARVESTER

Like the combine harvester above, the beet harvester combines several processes in one machine. In this case, the beet plant's leaves are removed, and the beet root is lifted from the ground by a mechanical fork. In the rotating cage wheel, the roots are shaken and spun to throw off stones and soil. The cleaned roots are collected in a hopper and often emptied straight into a truck trailer alongside the harvester.

Elevator takes beet from hopper to storage bin

Beet elevator

Beet hopper

Leaf elevator

Cage wheel

Soil and stones flung off

Guide wheel

Lifting fork

Guide skids

Topped beet in ground

Topping knife

Spiked roller

2 COMBINE

The crop is cut by the revolving wheel and cutter bar (1), pushed into the machine by the feeder (2), and taken by the transfer auger (3) to the main grain auger (4). The thresher separates the grain from the straw via distribution augers (5). A fan (6) blasts air through a series of sieves (7) to blow away the chaff. Unsorted grain is sent around again by the return cross auger (8). The threshed grain travels along the grain auger (9) and distribution auger (10) to the storage tank (11). The entire machine is powered by a diesel engine (12) and controlled by the driver in the cab (13).

Grain and straw

Grain

Straw

Air currents

3 GRAIN HANDLING

Grain is ground into flour, which is an ingredient of many foods such as breads, pastries and cakes. The grains are actually small seeds, which would otherwise grow into new plants. After the grain has been harvested (*see above*), it must be prevented from germinating (starting to grow) or going moldy, otherwise it would be of no use to the miller. The seeds are kept extremely dry, and in some cases in a special mixture of gases, before they are taken to the grinding mill.

Holding bin

Drying unit

Silo

Underground conveyor

121

4 BALER

Hay is cut dried grass, and it makes a nutritious food for farm animals. Straw is the leftover stems of grain plants – cereals such as wheat, oats, barley, and rye. The baler collects hay or straw, presses it into neat blocks, and ties the blocks with twine. Straw has many uses, from animal bedding to mats to mattress stuffing.

1 Crop is separated and packed into charge chamber

3 Hay is tied and ejected as a bale

2 Stuffer forks and plunger load hay and compress it into baling chamber

6 MILKING PARLOR

Mechanical milking parlors are regularly inspected by health experts to ensure the cleanest possible conditions. The milk is sucked from the cow's udder by a vacuum system, in the same way that a calf would suck the milk from its mother. The pulsator unit produces vibrations which massage the teat and encourage milk flow.

Vacuum pump

Interceptor trap

Flow gauge

Sanitary trap

Pulsator

Milk storage

7 PLOW

Today's plow has changed little from medieval times, although the pulling power is now usually a diesel-engined tractor! The blade cuts into the soil and the moldboard turns it over, ready for the new crop.

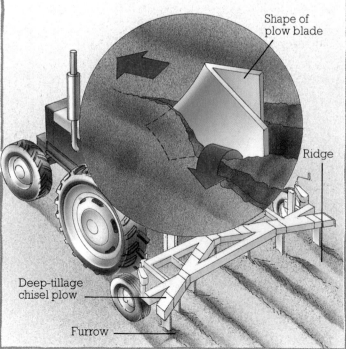

Shape of plow blade

Ridge

Deep-tillage chisel plow

Furrow

5 TRACTOR

The farm tractor is powered by a large diesel engine (page 89). A tractor is able to pull or push implements, such as plows and harrows. A large tractor can pull a 21-blade plow and cover 148 acres in one day.

In addition, there are take-off drive shafts which are set in motion using the extra gearshift in the cab. The take-off shafts drive other machines, such as separators or circular saws.

TRACTOR

Rear take-off shaft · Rear axles · Gearshift · Take-off shaft selector · Drive shaft · Gearbox · Front take-off shaft · Diesel engine

8 SEED DRILL

Jethro Tull's invention of the horse-drawn mechanized seed drill, in about 1701, brought great changes to agriculture. Rather than simply throwing seeds onto the soil, or planting them by hand, the drill inserted each seed to the correct depth in the soil and covered it over. Planting seeds in neat rows also paved the way for mechanical harvesters.

4-ROW SEED DRILL

1 Furrow cut
2 Seeds placed in furrow
3 Furrow filled

9 CROP SPRAYER

Herbicides kill weeds and other unwanted plants. Fungicides kill mildews, rusts and other unwanted fungi. Pesticides kill beetles, aphids and other harmful pests. Applications can be sprayed onto crops from the air without damaging the growing plants.

Low-altitude spray run

Half-circle turn with spray switched off

THE NATURAL WORLD

BIRDS 6

FISHES 3

PLANTS 1

MAMMALS 7

NATURAL CYCLES 8

REPTILES 5

STINGS AND POISONS 9

INSECTS AND ARACHNIDS 2

ECOLOGY 10

AMPHIBIANS 4

1 PLANTS

The living world can be studied in the same way as a machine, to see how the parts fit together and how they work. This is the science of ecology (page 128). Plants are vital since they feed animals. A plant absorbs minerals from the soil through its roots. It traps the energy in sunlight using its leaves. The minerals and energy are combined with carbon dioxide from the air to form new plant tissues during growth. The flower contains egg cells that are fertilized by pollen from another flower, and they develop into seeds. The seeds are spread by wind, water, or animals and grow into new plants.

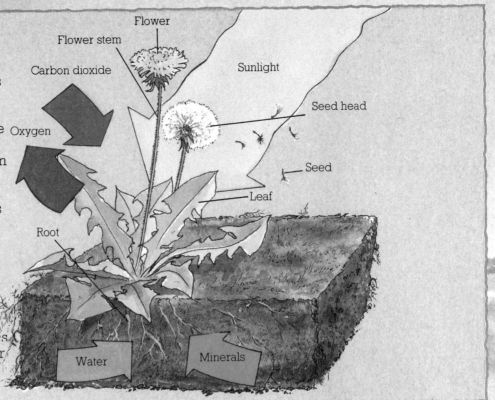

Flower
Flower stem
Carbon dioxide
Sunlight
Oxygen
Seed head
Seed
Leaf
Root
Water
Minerals

2 INSECTS AND ARACHNIDS

These small animals are among the most numerous on earth. All insects, including butterflies, beetles, grasshoppers, ants, bees, and flies, have six legs. Arachnids have eight legs and they include spiders, scorpions, mites and ticks. Both types have a hard outer casing, or exoskeleton, which protects the soft parts inside. As the creature grows, the old casing is shed regularly and replaced by a new, larger one.

Heart
Antenna
Wing
Eye
Nerve Gizzard Crop
Anus Gut
ARACHNID
INSECT

3 FISHES

Like other animals, a fish needs to take in oxygen and get rid of carbon dioxide. It uses the oxygen dissolved in water. The oxygen passes through the very thin coverings of the gill filaments into the blood just beneath. As the fish swims forward, a current of water flows over its gills. This ensures continuing supplies of oxygen, and the water carries away unwanted carbon dioxide.

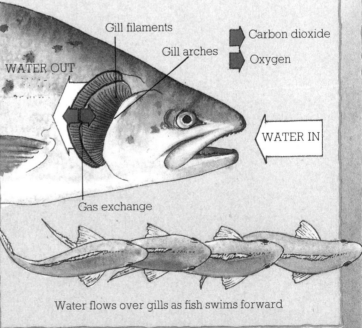

Gill filaments
Carbon dioxide
Gill arches
Oxygen
WATER OUT
WATER IN
Gas exchange

Water flows over gills as fish swims forward

4 AMPHIBIANS

Most amphibians have thin, moist skin that soon dries out, so they live in damp places or near water. They must return to water to lay their jelly-coated eggs, or spawn. The eggs hatch into young, called tadpoles, which live in water for the first few weeks and breathe using gills. As they grow, their gills disappear and they begin to breathe with lungs. Their body gradually changes to the adult form, a process called *metamorphosis*.

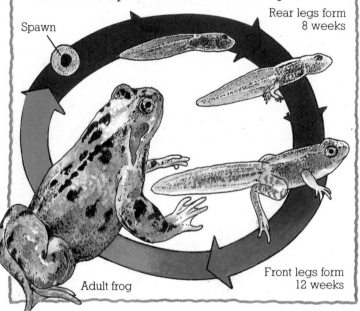

Spawn

Rear legs form 8 weeks

Front legs form 12 weeks

Adult frog

5 REPTILES

Unlike the amphibian egg, the reptile egg is enclosed in a tough, waterproof shell. Reptiles have scaly, waterproof skin. This means they can live entirely on land, unlike amphibians. Reptiles are not warm-blooded like birds and mammals, but they can keep their bodies relatively warm by basking in the sun when cold or cooling off in the shade when hot.

EARLY MORNING

Lizard absorbs sun's warmth

MIDDAY

Lizard cools in shade

6 BIRDS

Birds are the only animals with feathers. The feathers help to keep body warmth in, and they also overlap to form a broad, airtight wing surface for flight. A bird spends much time preening its feathers, getting rid of dirt and spreading waterproofing oils, to keep them in good condition. Like reptiles, birds lay shelled eggs. When the chicks first hatch they have no feathers, or only very small ones. They are cared for by their parents until they can fly.

Barb

Shaft

Barbule

Movement of wings in flight

Upstroke

FEATHER

Downstroke

7 MAMMALS

A mammal is a warm-blooded animal with fur that feeds its young on milk. Marsupial mammals have pouches, where the young live during their early growth and development. Marsupial mammals include kangaroos, koalas and opossums. The young of placental mammals develop in the womb, inside the mother's body.

Placental mother lacks pouch

Marsupial baby feeds and shelters in pouch

8 NATURAL CYCLES

Nature wastes nothing. Plants obtain their minerals and nutrients from the soil. They are eaten by herbivorous animals, such as cows, sheep, horses and rodents. Carnivores eat other animals; those which eat insects are called insectivores. As plants and animals die, their remains rot back into the soil again. Or they may become food for detritivores, such as maggots and beetle larvae. Natural recycling is an important part of ecology (page 128).

Animals communicate with each other in many ways. Wolves use facial expressions, body posture and tail position to convey their moods and intentions.

Reindeer

Wolves

Sparrowhawk

Flycatcher

Fly and maggots

Buzzard

Dead reindeer

9 STINGS AND POISONS

Various plants and animals have poisonous stings or bites. In plants the stings are for defense, to prevent animals from eating them. The spines of cacti and the thorns of rosebushes and brambles do a similar job. Some animals have a poisonous bite or sting for defense, such as scorpions and bees. Others use their poison to catch and subdue their prey. Among these are jellyfishes, coneshells, spiders, certain fishes such as the scorpionfish, and venomous snakes. The fangs of a snake work like a hypodermic needle (page 115) to inject the poison into the victim.

VIPER

Venom flows along channel in fang

Venom sac

Fang swings forward when striking

JELLYFISH

Barbs

Stinging fluid

Coiled thread

Thread fired outward

Nucleus

NETTLE

Stinging fluid

Hair breaks off, releasing fluid

10 ECOLOGY

Ecology is the study of how animals and plants live together: who eats what, who shelters where, and how minerals and nutrients are recycled in the living world. Shown here are only a few of the animals that live in and around a river. Each is adapted to a certain way of life. The *niche* of an animal or plant population describes its position in the web of nature – including its requirements for warmth, moisture, light or shade, food, shelter, nesting sites, and other conditions for survival.

Male stickleback guarding eggs in nest among reeds

Dragonfly larva eating tadpole

Beaver family at home in lodge, in lake

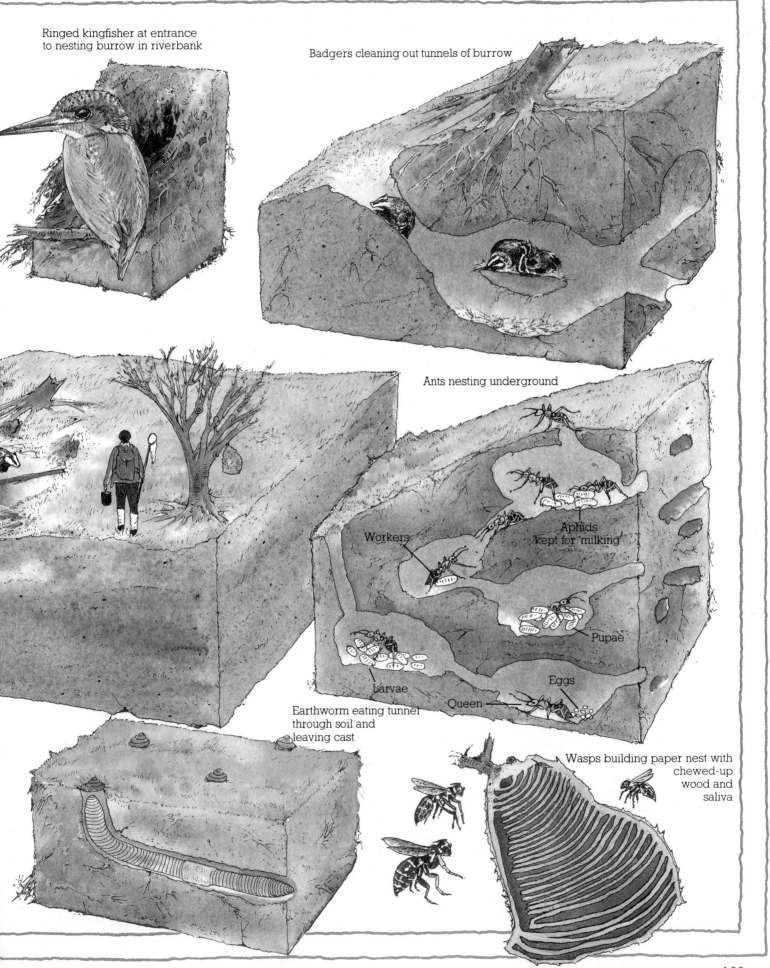

Ringed kingfisher at entrance to nesting burrow in riverbank

Badgers cleaning out tunnels of burrow

Ants nesting underground

Workers

Aphids kept for milking

Pupae

Larvae

Queen

Eggs

Earthworm eating tunnel through soil and leaving cast

Wasps building paper nest with chewed-up wood and saliva

ENTERTAINMENT

PIANO

STEREO MUSIC SYSTEM

VIDEO CAMERA AND PLAYER

TELEVISION

1 PIANO

Each piano key works as a simple lever that sets in motion a series of levers, catches, and springs. The result is that the damper lifts from the string as the hammer strikes it. As long as the key is held down, the damper stays away from the string. When the key is allowed to return, the damper comes back into contact with the string and stops its vibrations. A foot pedal moves all the dampers so that the strings continue to ring even after the keys return.

String

Damper

Repeat lever

Drop screw

Roller

Regulating button

Check

Jack

Hammer

Wippen

Key

TELEVISION

The color television tube has three *electron guns*: red, green, and blue. They shoot beams of electrons at the screen. The direction of the beams is controlled by electrically charged plates or deflector coils. The beams sweep across the screen to form a line and then move down the screen, sweeping line by line, to build up the picture. There are 25 or 30 complete pictures each second. Where each electron beam strikes the screen, it causes a corresponding color of phosphor strip to glow and give off light. When all three guns aim at the same place, each produces tiny spots of its own color. From a distance, the eye merges these spots of primary color and sees white. Where no electrons strike the screen, the eye sees black. The *chrominance* signals control the relative brightness of each color, while the *luminance* signal controls the overall brightness of all three colors.

Mask

Electron beams

Phosphor strips

Electron guns

Electrically charged focusing plates

Electron beams

Vacuum inside tube

Mask

Phosphor strips

Glass screen

VIDEO CAMERA AND PLAYER

A video camera does not use light to create a chemical change in photographic film, as in the ordinary camera (page 77). Instead, the light is focused onto a target plate that has a layer of *photoconductive* material. This is a material that conducts varying amounts of electricity according to the amount and color of light that shines onto it. The photoconductive material is scanned point-by-point across the plate by electronic circuitry, and the image on it is coded into a stream of electrical signals. These are recorded as tiny magnetized patches on magnetic tape – dozens of images each second. The tape is contained in a plastic case called a videocassette. When the tape is played, the playback head picks up the coded patches of magetism and converts them into electrical signals, which are fed to the television set. Sound is also recorded, in a narrow strip at the top of the tape.

Light rays from image

Lens

Target plate

Videotape cassette

Automatic loading poles pull tape from cassette

Erase head

Eyepiece

Signals to cassette

Audio head

Pinch roller

Feed spool

Take-up spool

The recording and playback heads in a video player are tilted at an angle. They record diagonally on the tape, using a scanning technique. Each diagonal track is of microscopic width. The head drum rotates, and the tape moves past it at $\frac{3}{4}$ inch per second.

Playback head is an angled, rotating drum

Blank tape

Diagonal tracks

Tape magnetized with picture and sound signals

4 STEREO MUSIC SYSTEM

A typical home stereo system consists of inputs, an amplifier, a control unit, and outputs. The inputs detect coded signals in a variety of forms, turn them into electrical signals, and feed them to the amplifier. For example, the radio tuner detects signals broadcast as radio waves, using its antenna. In the vinyl disk record player, the signals are coded as bumps and waves in a V-shaped groove. In a compact disk player, they are in the form of microscopic bumps and pits which are read by a laser beam. In an audio cassette, the signals are tiny patches of magnetism on the tape. The signals are altered by the tone controls, made stronger in the amplifier, and then fed to the outputs – usually loudspeakers or headphones.

Cassette unit Compact disk unit Phonograph unit

Loudspeakers

Amplifier

Pinch roller

Record-playback head

Erase head

Head pressure pad

Take-up spool

AUDIO CASSETTE

Feed spool

Lenses

Semireflective mirror

COMPACT DISK

Laser beam source

Close-up of CD surface

Photodiode

Signals to amplifier

MAGNETIC PICK-UP FOR VINYL DISK

Signals to amplifier

Coils in magnetic field

Permanent magnet

Pivot

Stylus

Close-up of vinyl disk

Signals coded as wavy V-shaped groove

Vibrations from groove move stylus

ROCK CONCERT

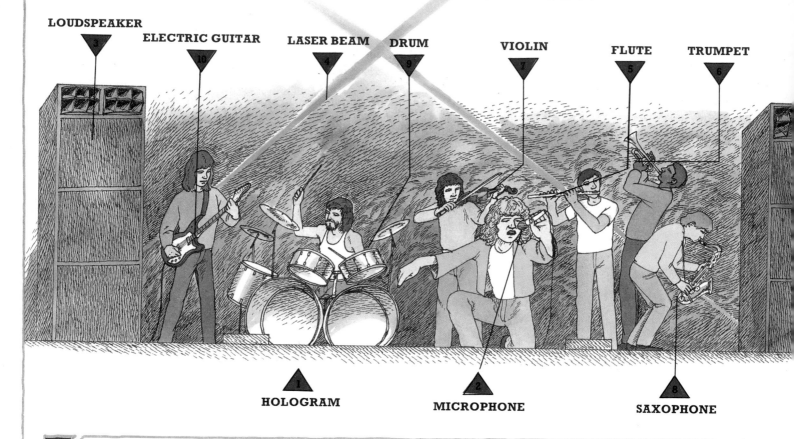

LOUDSPEAKER 3

ELECTRIC GUITAR 10

LASER BEAM 4

DRUM 9

VIOLIN 7

FLUTE 5

TRUMPET 6

HOLOGRAM 1

MICROPHONE 2

SAXOPHONE 8

1 HOLOGRAM

A hologram exists on a flat sheet, like an ordinary photograph. But when viewed under certain conditions, the image is three-dimensional and has depth. A hologram is recorded on special holography photographic film. One part of a laser beam, the object beam, shines on the object to be photographed and is reflected by the object onto the plate. The other part, the reference beam, is split off by a partially reflecting mirror and shines directly onto the plate. The plate records the pattern made by the two beams interfering with each other. When the hologram is illuminated by a reference laser beam, the exact pattern of the object beam is recreated.

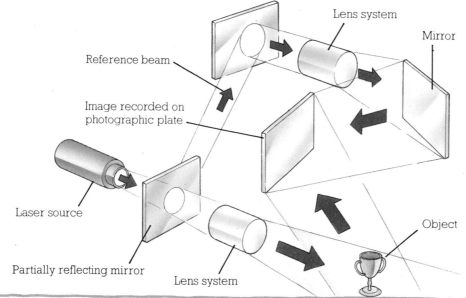

Lens system

Mirror

Reference beam

Image recorded on photographic plate

Laser source

Partially reflecting mirror

Lens system

Object

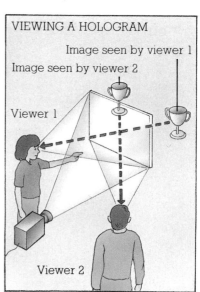

VIEWING A HOLOGRAM

Image seen by viewer 1

Image seen by viewer 2

Viewer 1

Viewer 2

2 MICROPHONE

A moving-coil microphone uses the principle of *inductance*. Sound waves vibrate the diaphragm, which is linked to a small coil of wire. As the coil moves in a magnetic field, small amounts of electricity are induced in its wiring and are fed to the amplifier.

Cover

Diaphragm

Coil attached to diaphragm

Magnets

Vibrating coil creates electric current

Signals to amplifier

3 LOUDSPEAKER

The speaker works in a way opposite to the microphone (*left*). Varying amounts of electricity from the amplifier travel through the coil attached to the loudspeaker cone. This coil is in the field of a strong permanent magnet and it vibrates as the electrical signals change. The vibrations move the cone, which vibrates the air and creates sound waves.

Wires bringing signals to coil

Cone vibrates

Permanent magnet   Coil

Midrange horn

Midrange cabinet

Path of sound waves

High-frequency bullet radiators

Low-frequency bass reflex cabinet

4 LASER BEAM

High-voltage electricity passes through a glass tube containing a mixture of gases, such as helium and neon. The electricity stimulates the gas atoms to give off tiny packets of light called photons. These stimulate other atoms to emit photons. Mirrors reflect most of the light back into the gas for further amplification. A partially silvered mirror at one end allows out a narrow, parallel beam of intensely bright, pure, single-color light – the laser beam. "Laser" stands for Lightwave Amplification by Stimulated Emission of Radiation.

Mirror

Active medium

Beam

Power source

Mirror

Light intensified between mirrors

5 ▶ FLUTE

A certain volume and shape of air resonates at its natural frequency of vibration to produce a musical tone. You can demonstrate this by blowing across the top of an empty bottle. The air inside resonates to give a hollow, humming tone. Half-fill the bottle with water and blow again – less air means a higher tone. A flute works in a similar way. The player blows across the hole in the mouthpiece. The keys open holes in the flute body, which changes the size and shape of air vibrated, thereby altering the tone produced.

Mouthpiece

Mouth hole

Finger keys

Standard 13-hole cylindrical body

Foot joint

Blowing over mouth of empty bottle has same effect

6 ▶ TRUMPET

Like the flute, the trumpet relies on the resonating quality of a volume of air. The player uses his or her lips to produce a "buzzing" in the mouthpiece, which vibrates the column of air inside the instrument. The brass bore is really one long tube about 50 inches in length, curved and folded into a more compact size and shape. Each key opens a valve that alters the distance the air travels, changing the tone slightly.

Mouthpiece

Valves

Piston

Straight air column

Valve closed

Extra loop of air created

Spring

Valve open

7 ▶ VIOLIN

As the violinist draws the bow across the strings, they vibrate and set in motion vibrations in the surrounding air. In turn, these vibrations make the violin's belly soundboard resonate and amplify the tone. The very best violins such as those made by Stradivarius are made from specially selected woods and assembled with supreme craftsmanship.

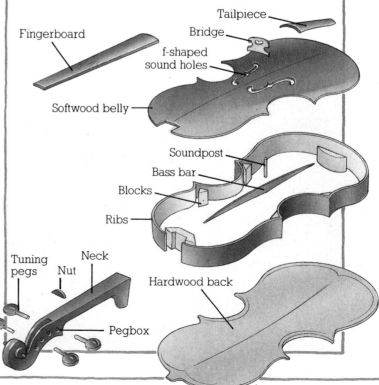

Fingerboard

Tailpiece

Bridge

f-shaped sound holes

Softwood belly

Soundpost

Bass bar

Blocks

Ribs

Tuning pegs

Nut

Neck

Hardwood back

Pegbox

8 SAXOPHONE

This instrument was invented by Adolphe Sax in the 1840s. A reed placed in the mouthpiece vibrates as air is blown over it. The vibrations create sound waves that resonate in the body and bell. As in a flute or oboe, keys alter the tones by changing the amount of air that vibrates.

Mouthpiece

Crook

Reed

Reed vibrates

Neckpiece

Bell

Upper stack keys

Bell keys

Lower stack keys

9 DRUM

The drum is one of the simplest musical instruments. Yet a good drummer can obtain varied sounds by altering the tension (tightness) of the drumhead, hitting it in different places and using various strikers such as ordinary drumsticks, wire or bristle brushes, or felt-padded hammerhead sticks.

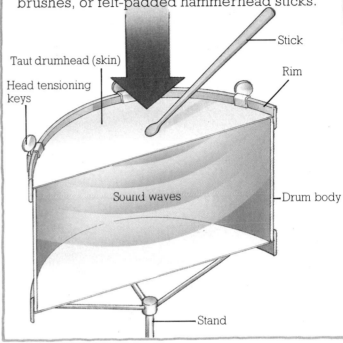

Taut drumhead (skin)

Head tensioning keys

Stick

Rim

Sound waves

Drum body

Stand

10 ELECTRIC GUITAR

A guitar is a stringed instrument that works in the same basic way as a violin. The string vibrates to give a tone according to its length. As the fingers press just behind the frets, shortening the vibrating part of the string, the tone becomes higher. In an acoustic guitar, the strings produce sound waves which are amplified by the resonating guitar body.

In an electric guitar, the metal strings vibrate in the magnetic field of the pick-ups. The vibrations alter the amounts of electricity in the wire coils of the pick-ups, creating electrical signals that travel along the lead to the amplifier.

Guitar body

Magnetic pick-ups

Neck

Machine head

Tuning keys

Fretboard

Frets

Metal string

Metal string vibrates when plucked

Pick-up coil

Magnetic field distorted

Bridge

Tone and volume controls

Pick-up selector switch

Magnet

Electric signals generated

Socket for lead to amplifier

THE FILM SET

MOVIE CAMERA ▼ 2

CINERAMA ▼ 1

SPECIAL EFFECTS ▼ 5

MOVIE PROJECTOR ▼ 7

LIGHTING ▼ 6

MOVIE FILM ▼ 3

EDITING ▼ 4

1

CINERAMA

A single movie projector shining onto a large, flat screen cannot show clearly the objects near the edge of the screen. Neither can viewers sitting to one side see the other side of the screen clearly. But with the curved Cinerama screen, three co-ordinated projectors show different parts of the scene at exactly the same time and the picture "wraps around" the viewer.

Screen

Multiple loudspeakers for sound

Three synchronized 35-mm projectors

Object — Curved screen

Viewer —

2 MOVIE CAMERA

Inside a movie camera, a revolving mirror shutter directs the light along two alternative paths, more than 20 times each second. One path is into the viewfinder (*below left*). The other is onto the film, through the film gate (*below right*). Each exposure records the scene as a separate picture on the roll of film as the film is pulled past the film gate by the motor and sprocket drive (*below*).

Film rolls

Shutter

Light reflected through viewfinder

Film plane

Prism

Lens

Shutter

Matte box

Front effects stage

Prime lens

Alternative lens

Prism

Viewfinder eyepiece

Film gate

Light rays on film

Shutter revolves

3 MOVIE FILM

Cinematic (movie) film is wound onto a reel in a lightproof cartridge or magazine. This clips onto the camera (*above*) so that the film travels past the film gate. The teeth on the drive sprockets fit into the rows of holes along each side of the film, and the drive motor is linked to the revolving mirror shutter. The film has three light-sensitive layers, and each layer reacts to light of a certain color.

Blue

Green

Red

Sensitive layers

Sprocket holes

Single frame of film

Image area

Soundtrack

4 ▸ EDITING

Few movies are recorded from start to finish on one film roll in one camera. When editing, the filmmaker chooses which individual pictures, or frames, of film should follow each other. The frames are cut up and joined together ("spliced") into the new sequence using glue.

Unwanted frame identified

5 ▸ SPECIAL EFFECTS

Filmmakers use many kinds of special effects to create scenes that do not exist in real life. One method is to film people through a hole in a fake background of painted scenery, called a matte. The people might look as though they are in a huge restaurant, when in fact they are at one table and the rest of the view is painted onto the matte. Another method is to film a person against a blue background, using either camera filters or film that cannot record the blue color. Another camera records a different background. The two views are blended together before being shown to the viewer. This technique is often used for television weather reports, to show the weather map on one camera combined with the weathercaster on another.

6 ▸ LIGHTING

There are many different kinds of light sources, such as the fluorescent tube (page 17) and the laser beam (page 135).

The light bulb is also called the incandescent lamp. It is made of a thin coil of special resistance wire containing the metal tungsten, which can withstand very high temperatures. The wire glows brightly, at a temperature of more than 4500°F, when electricity flows along it. A special gas mixture inside the glass, or a vacuum of no gas at all, prevents the wire from burning out too quickly. Very powerful incandescent lamps are used to light film sets, so that the cameras can pick up all the details of the actors, objects, and scenery. These lamps are rated at many thousands of watts of electricity, compared to the typical home light bulb of about 60, 100, or 150 watts.

"Barn door" light deflectors

Air vents

Light bulb

INCANDESCENT LIGHT BULB

Inert gas

Filament

Filament support

Electrical contacts

Scenery painted on matte

Actors

Glass matte screen

Key area

Background

Weathercaster

Blue screen

Weather map

Camera 1

Camera 2

Blending box

Viewer sees composite image

MOVIE PROJECTOR

The source of light in a typical movie projector is the continuous and intensely bright spark of a carbon arc lamp. The spark leaps between two carbon rods. As the carbon burns away, electrical motor drives move the rods along slowly to replace it. Heat shields protect the film from the high-temperature arc. The light shines through the film in the film guide, then through a system of lenses and across the movie theater onto the screen. The soundtrack is picked up either by an optical reader, if it was recorded in the form of light patterns, or by a magnetic pick-up if it was recorded on magnetic tape.

Film spool

Projection lens

Carbon-arc-lamp light source

Sprockets

Sound drum

Loudspeaker

Amplifier

AMUSEMENT PARK

MAGLEV TRAIN 6

ELECTRICITY GENERATION 7

BUMPER CAR 3

ROLLER COASTER 4

TEST-YOUR-STRENGTH 2

FLYING WALL 5

AIR GUN 1

1 AIR GUN

The energy that speeds the air gun pellet on its way does not come from a chemical explosion, as in an ordinary gun bullet. It comes from the muscles of the shooter, who pulls back the barrel and lever in order to compress the air and the spring inside the gun body.

Chamber pulled back

Pellet loaded

Spring compressed

Barrel compresses spring when pulled down

Air pressure shoots pellet down barrel

Chamber shoots forward

Pulling trigger releases spring

TEST-YOUR-STRENGTH

Like the air gun (*opposite page*), energy to work this device comes from the competitor's muscles. A simple lever combines with the physical principle that every action has a reaction (page 95). The hammer crashes down on one end of the lever, lifting the other end, which knocks the clapper upward. Friction and the force of gravity between the clapper and the rail quickly slow the clapper, so that most hits do not ring the bell at the top.

BUMPER CAR

The sliding contact, contact arm, car motor and metal front wheel form part of an electrical circuit, between the metal screen in the roof and the metal floor of the bumper rink. People standing on the floor are too far away from the roof screen to be in danger of completing the circuit themselves – and being electrocuted. The motor is mounted on the front wheel and turns with it, to avoid the need for complex rack-and-pinion steering as in a car (page 87). As the bumper car moves, the sliding contact rubs along the roof screen. Sparks fly between the contact and screen when there are small gaps.

Rail

Score scale

Clapper

Hammer

Strike peg

Lever

Sliding contact

Metal screen

Contact arm carries electricity from metal screen to car

Steering wheel

½ hp electric motor drives front wheel

Drive belt

All-around bumper

Rubber rear wheels

Metal front wheel carries electricity from car to metal floor

4 ROLLER COASTER

The laws of physics state that a moving object will continue in a straight line unless acted on by an outside force to change its speed or direction. As the riders in a roller coaster loop the loop, they are moving in a circle and are therefore changing direction from a straight line. The force causing this to happen is the *centripetal* force, which acts toward the center of the circle, continually pushing the riders inward. The reaction to centripetal force is felt when the riders are pressed into their seats.

Reaction to centripetal force

Car accelerates down slope and around loop

Gravitational force

Roller-coaster car

Teeth on car slot into chain

Chain drive

5 FLYING WALL

The flying wall works in a way similar to the roller coaster. The motion in this case is in a horizontal circle rather than a vertical one. The centripetal force acts to make the riders go around in a circle rather than along in a straight line. As a reaction to this force, they press against the revolving drum wall and stay there – even when the floor is lowered from under their feet! The old term *centrifugal* force is no longer used to explain these types of movements.

Gravitational force keeps riders pressed against floor

Hydraulic rams

Floor lowered by rams

Tendency of riders to go in a straight line creates a force that keeps them pressed against a wall

6 MAGLEV TRAIN

A magnet has two poles, north and south. Like poles repel (push apart). Unlike poles attract (pull together). The maglev (magnetic levitation) train uses this principle. Electromagnets in the train base and the single rail create very powerful magnetic fields. Their poles are arranged so that the train and rail repel each other. The upper repelling force lifts, or levitates, the train so it runs on a bed of air. The lower repelling force keeps the train steady as it travels along.

Electromagnets in train

Electromagnets in rail

ATTRACTING AND REPELLING

Like poles repel

Unlike poles attract

N   N

S   N

7 ELECTRICITY GENERATION

When a wire moves in a magnetic field, an electric current is induced (page 135) in the wire. In the direct-current (DC) generator, wire coils spin between two strong permanent magnets. The electricity induced in the coils reverses its direction as each part of the coil moves from the north to south pole of the magnets, but gaps in the *commutator* mean that a steady direct current is produced. In the alternating-current (AC) generator, each end of the wire coil has a separate brush, so that the current reverses – alternates – with each turn.

DC GENERATOR (DYNAMO)

N   S

Permanent magnets

Wire coil of armature

Brushes

Direct current

AC GENERATOR (ALTERNATOR)

N   S

Rotating magnets

Wire coil of armature

Brushes and slip rings

Alternating current

GLOSSARY

Note: The following descriptions aim to explain, in a simple way, the terms as they are used in this book. Some of the terms have more restricted scientific meanings or wider everyday usages. Consult a good dictionary for these.

Airfoil The specially curved shape of an aircraft wing, when viewed from the side, that produces lift as air flows past it.

Amp (ampere) A unit of measurement for electrical current – the rate of flow of electricity (see also Volt, Watt).

Amplifier An electronic device that makes an electrical signal more powerful or stronger.

Anchor A heavy weight, sometimes designed to stick in soil or mud, which stops an object such as a ship from drifting away.

Annealing involves heating and then cooling a substance under closely controlled conditions, to make it strong and tough without being too brittle.

Annealing lehr A tunnel-shaped oven for annealing glass.

Anode In an electrical circuit, the positive electrode (see also Cathode and Electrode).

Arc The bridge formed when electricity leaps across a small gap in a circuit, usually producing light, noise and heat as a spark.

Archimedes screw A long ramp wrapped around a central shaft, like a corkscrew. As it turns it pushes material along its length.

Atom The smallest particle of a substance that still has the chemical properties of that substance (see also Electron, Neutron, Proton).

Balance When an object is supported at or below its center of gravity, so that the force of gravity does not pull more on one side and tip it over.

Barometer An instrument for measuring air pressure, used in meteorology and in some types of altimeter ("height-meter") in aircraft.

Battery

Battery The common name for an electrical cell that makes electricity by chemical reactions. A true battery is really a number of cells joined together.

Archimedes screw

Bevel gear A gear with sloping conical teeth, usually meshing at right angles with a similar gear.

Bimetallic strip Two joined pieces of metal that bend with changes in temperature because they expand at different rates.

Bulb A light bulb is a hollow glass globe containing a wire filament that glows brightly as electricity passes through it.

Cam An uneven ring on an axle or shaft that presses on or moves another part of the machine as it rotates.

Camber The slope or inclined bank of a broad surface. A cambered road allows the rain to drain away and gives better cornering on bends.

Cantilever Part of a structure, such as a bridge, that projects outward from its support as an overhang and helps to support the structure.

Cathode In an electrical circuit, the negative electrode (see also Anode and Electrode).

Center of gravity The point at which all an object's weight can be thought to be concentrated, so that it balances if supported below this point.

Centrifugal force An outward force which is often thought to act on an object going in a circle (see Centripetal force).

Centripetal force The force which acts to keep an object moving in a circle. Twirl a ball on a string and the pull in the string represents the centripetal force.

Chrominance The part of a television signal that controls the relative brightness of the three colors: red, green and blue.

Circuit In electricity, a series of conductors joined into a loop, around which the electricity flows.

Cold-blooded See Warm-blooded.

Condenser A device for condensing a substance, changing it from gas to liquid.

Conductor A substance that allows electricity to pass through it easily. Most metals are good conductors (see also Resistance).

Cracking In an oil refinery, separating the crude oil into its many ingredients by heating and then condensing at different temperatures.

Crank and crankshaft A device for changing a rotary (turning) motion to an oscillating (back-and-forth) one, or vice versa. The shaft has one or more bars, called cranks, fixed to it at an angle. These are usually linked to other bars by pivots. As the shaft turns round, the ends of the bars travel backward and forward (see also Oscillation).

Damping Cushioning or evening out bumps and vibrations.

Diaphragm A disk or sheet of flexible material which, for example, bends to operate a valve or suck in a fluid.

Drill A length of hard material such as steel, with a sharpened end (the drill bit), turned by a machine such as an electric motor. It gouges out a circular hole as it twists around.

Electricity A type of energy involving electrons or similar particles with an electrical charge. In an electrical circuit,

Drill

electrons flow from the negative terminal of the battery to the positive one (see Electron).

Electric motor A machine that changes electrical energy into the energy of spinning motion.

Electrode In an electrical circuit, the part that either collects (anode) or emits (cathode) the moving electrons which form the electric current.

Electrolysis Producing a chemical reaction using electricity. Usually it refers to splitting a substance into its constituent parts by dissolving it and then passing electricity through the solution.

Electromagnet A magnet which is magnetized only when electricity passes through the wire coil around it.

Electromagnet

Electron One type of particle that makes up atoms. The electron has a negative charge and orbits the central part of the atom, the nucleus (see also Atom, Neutron, Proton).

Electrostatic Concerning static electricity, when electrical charges are at rest on or in an object rather than flowing through it as an electric current.

Element (heater) Special wire that resists the flow of electricity, becoming hot in the process.

Escapement In a clock, the mechanism that allows the stored energy in the spring to "escape" in small, regular amounts.

Feedback Information coming back into a system about the way it is changing. One example is a thermostat, which shuts down the central heating system when the temperature rises above a certain level (see Thermostat).

Fertilization In reproduction, when a male cell (sperm) joins with a female cell (egg), ready to grow into a new individual.

Filter A fine net or similar material that removes solid impurities from a fluid or separates larger particles from smaller ones.

Foundation The secure and stable base of a structure, such as a skyscraper or bridge, that stops it from sinking into the earth or toppling over.

Four-stroke engine An internal combustion engine driven by pistons that have a complete power cycle every four strokes: down, up, down, up.

Friction The heat and wear produced when two surfaces rub together as they move past each other. Friction can be minimized by lubricating oil.

Fulcrum The pivot point of a lever.

Furnace A very hot chamber or oven.

Fulcrum

Gear A wheel edged with V-shaped teeth, cogs or notches that mesh with those of a similar wheel or interlock with the row of holes in a chain.

Gene A set of instructions, in the form of a chemical code (DNA), which controls the building or working of part of the body.

Two interlocking gear wheels

Generator A machine that produces electricity from another form of energy, such as moving water (hydroelectricity) or the chemical energy in a fuel.

Germination The sprouting of a seed and the beginning of its growth as a plant.

Gravity The force of attraction between objects. Usually used for the attraction of the earth on objects near its surface, pulling them down toward its center.

Gyroscope A spinning wheel with a heavy rim, on a set of pivots, which tends to resist change in position (see Inertia).

Heat exchanger A device for transferring heat from one substance to another, for example, when hot exhaust gases pre-warm the cool air coming into a combustion engine.

Hormone A type of "chemical messenger," made by a gland, which travels around in the blood and controls the way certain organs work.

Hydraulics The science of the force of motion of liquids. In a hydraulic machine, fluid – usually an oil – is used to transmit pressure along pipes from one part to another.

Hydroelectricity Electricity generated from the energy of moving water.

Hydrophone A type of

Hydraulic piston

microphone designed to pick up sounds under water.

Inductance The process by which a magnetic field and nearby conducting wire move relative to each other, creating an electric current in the wire.

Inertia The tendency of objects to stay still or keep moving as they are, resisting any change in position or motion.

Insect An animal with six legs, a three-part body, and a hard outer casing called an exoskeleton.

Internal combustion engine A machine that changes the chemical energy in fuel, such as gasoline, into the energy of a turning shaft, by small explosions (combustions) in an enclosed space, the cylinder.

Jack A lifting machine that raises a heavy load by small amounts, using a smaller effort moving a much greater total distance.

Jet A fast-moving stream of fluid, such as water or air. A jet engine produces a fast-moving stream of hot gases from its exhaust.

Jack

Key A specially shaped object, usually metal, that fits into and opens a lock.

Laser A powerful pure-color beam of light produced from a gas or crystal, by the process of

Key and lock

Lightwave **A**mplification by the **S**timulated **E**mission of **R**adiation.

Lens A specially shaped piece of glass, usually with curved surfaces, that brings light rays together (convergence) or spreads them apart (divergence).

Lever In its simplest form, a rigid bar that pivots on its

Lever

fulcrum or "hinge." Press down on one side, and the other side moves up.

Light A form of energy, as electromagnetic waves, that we can see with our eyes.

Luminance The part of a television signal which controls the overall brightness of the image.

Magnet A piece of material, usually iron-based metal, that has a magnetic field around it and can attract or repel other magnets (see also Electromagnet).

Magnet

Magnetic field Lines of magnetic force around a magnet, tending to attract or repel other magnets and attract magnetic objects (see also Inductance).

Matte A frame or border used to blank out part of a scene or to show painted scenery when making films or TV programs.

Nerve A fiber of living tissue that carries electrical nerve signals in an animal in the way that a wire conducts electricity.

Neutron One type of particle that makes up atoms. The

neutron has no charge and is in the central part of the atom, the nucleus (see also Atom, Electron, Proton).

Niche In ecology, the position of a living thing in the natural world, including its requirements for food, light, warmth and shelter.

Nut In engineering, a flat-sided object with a hole in its center that is grooved for screwing onto a bolt.

Nut

Oscillation Movement back and forth.

Otoscope A light-and-lens device used by a doctor to examine the inside of the ear.

Oxidation The chemical reaction when a substance combines with oxygen, such as rusting (see also Reduction). The process involves a loss of electrons.

Peristalsis Wavelike muscular squeezing of a tube inside an animal, such as the gut, which pushes along the contents.

Pig iron Fairly impure iron straight from the furnace, containing relatively large amounts of carbon and other impurities.

Pinion A small gearwheel that meshes with a larger one (see also Rack and pinion).

Piston A (usually) cylindrical object that moves up and down

inside a hollow cylinder, as in a car engine.

Piston

Plow A curved blade pulled through the soil, that churns it up and turns it over.

Polarization When the up-and-down motions of waves all happen in the same direction. Without polarization, the ups and downs occur at any angle (sideways, diagonally and so on).

Pollen Tiny grains containing male cells, made by the male parts of a flower, which fertilize the female parts to form seeds (see Fertilization).

Pressure The force acting on a certain area. The same total force pressing on a surface of 10 square yards would have 10 times the pressure if it pressed on one square yard.

Primary colors A set of three colors from which all other colors of the spectrum can be obtained, by mixing. For light rays they are usually red, green and blue. For printing inks they are yellow, magenta and cyan.

Prism A piece of transparent material, usually glass or clear plastic, that changes the direction of light rays by reflection or refraction. Some prisms are used to separate white light into the different colors of the spectrum.

Program The sequence of instructions inside a computer, telling it what to do with the information fed in.

Propeller A device with a central shaft and angled blades that "screw" through a gas or liquid and propel something along, such as a boat or plane.

Proton One type of particle that makes up atoms. The proton has a positive charge and is in the central part of the atom, the nucleus (see also Atom, Electron, Neutron).

Pulley A grooved wheel on a central axle or shaft, either free to turn on it or fixed so that it turns with the shaft.

Quartz crystal A crystal made of quartz (silicon dioxide), which vibrates at a certain frequency when electricity passes through it. The vibrations can be used to control an electronic time-keeping circuit.

Rack and pinion The rack is a bar with a row of teeth that mesh with the teeth on a pinion (small gearwheel). As the pinion turns, the bar slides along.

Radar (**RA**dio **D**etection **A**nd **R**anging) Navigating or detecting objects using radio waves or their reflections (see also Sonar).

Ratchet A bar with a point (pawl) that presses against sloped teeth on a wheel. The wheel can turn only one way. The point jams against the teeth and stops the wheel from turning the other way.

Receiver A device that detects waves or signals, such as a radio receiver that picks up radio waves.

Rectifier A device that allows electricity to pass in one direction only. It converts alternating current to direct current.

Reduction The chemical reaction when an oxygen-containing substance loses its oxygen (see also Oxidation). The process involves a gain of electrons.

Reflection The effect when rays bounce off an object, as when light rays are cast back from a mirror or sound waves bounce off a wall to give an echo.

Reflex An automatic response by the body before it registers in the brain, such as pulling your finger away from a hot object.

Refraction The bending of rays of light at the place where they go from one substance into another, such as from air into the glass of a lens.

Resistance A material's degree of opposition to the flow of electricity. Electrical insulators such as plastics have very high resistance (see also Conductor).

Resonance The full and echoing sound heard when vibrations travel through a hollow chamber and bounce off hard materials.

Robot A machine that can carry out a fairly complex task, usually in the manner of a person, such as spraying a car body with paint. Modern robots are usually computer-controlled.

Satellite An object that goes around (orbits) another, usually larger, object. The moon is a natural satellite of the earth. Hundreds of artificial satellites orbit the earth.

Siphon An upside-down U tube that draws a continuous stream of fluid from a higher to a lower level. Fluid in the higher and shorter leg is pushed up and around the U bend by the force of the atmosphere on the upper surface.

Skeleton The hard, stiff framework of an animal or structure. In humans, it is formed of bones. In an insect it consists of the hard outer shell or exoskeleton.

Sonar (**SO**und and **NA**vigation **R**anging) Navigating or detecting objects using sound waves or their reflections (see also Radar).

Sound waves Patterns of vibrating molecules which travel through the air and which we hear as sounds.

Spindle A thin central axle or shaft in a wheel, bobbin, etc.

Spring

Spring A coiled device, usually made of metal or special plastic. It can be squeezed or stretched but always tries to return to its normal length.

Suspension bridge A bridge in which the deck hangs (is suspended) from main cables strung between supporting towers.

Switch A device that opens or closes a gap in an electrical circuit to stop the electricity or allow it to flow.

Theodolite An instrument that measures angles, used in surveying.

Thermostat A switch that turns

on or off a heating or cooling system to keep the temperature roughly constant.

Thrust A propelling force, as when hot gases rush from the back of a jet engine and cause the engine to react by being pushed forward.

Torque When a force acts in a circular direction, to turn or twist.

Transformer An electrical device that increases or decreases the voltage, with a corresponding fall or rise in the current (see Amp, Volt).

Transmitter A device that sends out waves or signals, such as a radio transmitter that emits radio waves.

Turbine A machine with angled

Turbine
blades mounted on a central shaft, like a fan. Fluid (such as water or hot gases) moving past the blades makes them spin.

Turbofan A type of jet engine that has a very large fanlike turbine at the front.

Two-stroke engine An internal combustion engine driven by pistons that have a complete power cycle every two strokes: up, down.

Universal joint Two U-shaped joints pivoted together so that one shaft can transmit its turning motion to another shaft which is at an angle to it.

Valve A device that lets a

substance flow one way but not the other (nonreturn valve), or that controls the rate of flow of a substance, such as water or air.

Volt A unit of measurement for the potential difference of electricity, which can be thought of as its "pushing strength" around the circuit (see also Amp, Watt).

Warm-blooded Referring to an animal that makes heat inside its body by chemical reactions and keeps a steady temperature independent of the surroundings. Cold-blooded animals do not make their own heat and must absorb it from the surroundings.

Warp In weaving, the yarns that are stretched along the length of the loom and between which the weft (filler) yarn passes on the shuttle.

Watt A unit of measurement of power. In an electrical system it is equal to volts multiplied by amps (see also Amp, Volt).

Wedge A form with two tapering sides or edges that meet in a V, used for forcing apart two surfaces when pushed between them.

Weft In weaving, the filler yarn carried by the shuttle. It threads its way between alternating sets of warp yarns.

Valve open (top) and closed (above)

Weld A joint made by melting two substances (usually metals) and allowing them to run together before they cool and solidify.

Wheel A disk-shaped object mounted on a central shaft or axle. The wheel is either fixed to the axle or free to spin on it.

X-rays Rays that are part of the electromagnetic spectrum, of a much shorter wavelength than light rays. They are given off when a suitable substance is bombarded with electrons (see Electron).

Zipper

Zipper A fastening device in which two rows of teeth are brought together so that they interlock.

Answer to question on page 30:
The total number of possible combinations is 10,000.

INDEX